I leaned back and closed my eyes.

First I imagined myself handing the check over to Mum and Dad. That should stop them rowing. All the press would want to know me, I'd be given a top makeover, my photo would be on the front of all the magazines. Everyone at school would be so jealous when my single went straight to number one. I'd win an award at the Grammys; in fact I'd present an award with my new best friend Kylie Minogue. I'd be a stone thinner and wearing an amazing sparkly designer dress and shoes, my hair would be perfectly straight for a change and afterward I'd go to an all-celebrity party with Robbie and Eminem and Madonna. Ohmigod, I thought as I folded the paper away, here I go again. The teachers were right—I *am* a dreamer.

The Princess of Pop

Cathy Hopkins

Simon Pulse
New York   London   Toronto   Sydney

First Simon Pulse edition May 2004

Copyright © 2002 by Cathy Hopkins
Originally published in Great Britain as *Truth, Dare, Kiss or Promise: Pop Princess* in 2002 by Piccadilly Press Ltd.

Published by arrangement with Piccadilly Press Ltd.

SIMON PULSE
An imprint of Simon & Schuster
Children's Publishing Division
1230 Avenue of the Americas
New York, NY 10020

Printed in the United States of America
4 6 8 10 9 7 5 3

Library of Congress Control Number 2003113058

ISBN 0-689-87002-7

Thanks as always to Brenda Gardner, Yasemin Uçar,
and the lovely team at Piccadilly; to Rosemary Bromley
at Juvenilia; and Becca Crewe, Alice Elwes,
Jenni Herzberg, and Olivia McDonnell for all
their e-mails in answer to my questions.

Grease Mania

"ARGHHHHHHHHHHHHHH," I groaned as I walked into the living room at Cat's house. "Not you as well. I can't stand it."

Cat looked up from the sofa. "What? What's the matter?"

I pointed at the TV screen. "*That*. That video of *Grease*. Everywhere I've been today, *everyone*'s got it on—Lia, Mac's watching it at Squidge's . . . I can't get away from it. What is wrong with everyone?"

Actually, I thought, that should be: What's wrong with me? All my mates were excited by the prospect of our school putting on *Grease* as the end-of-term show. The whole school was, in fact. Everyone except me. But I had my reasons.

Cat sprang up and went into a dance routine. "'Summer loving, had me a blast,'" she sang along with John Travolta on the TV. "Oh, come on, Becca.

It's the first time ever that we're doing something decent for the end-of-term show. Makes a change from all those boring fairy stories we usually do."

I flopped down on the sofa. "I suppose this means that you're going up for a part?"

"Yeah," said Cat, sitting next to me and flicking off the video. "I thought about going for the part of Rizzo. What do you think?"

"Perfect," I said. She would be. She looks the part exactly—small, with dark hair like Stockard Channing in the movie. And she can sing as well. "Yeah. And Rizzo has the best song, I think."

"'I could flirt with all the guys,'" sang Cat.

"'Tease and tantalize,'" I joined in.

"What about you, Bec? Don't you want to be in it?"

I shrugged. "Haven't really thought about it." Actually, that was a lie. I had thought about it. We've got this new drama teacher at school called Miss Segal and she's really cool for a teacher. It was her idea to put on something more contemporary, and suddenly everyone in the school wants to be in the show. Secretly I do as well, but I'd like to play the lead, Sandy. She was played by

Olivia Newton-John in the film, though, so they'll be looking for someone skinny and blond. And that's the problem. I've got red hair, and nobody in their right mind would ever use the word "skinny" to describe me. "Curvy" is what Cat says. "Fat" is what I say. My secret fantasy is that I lose half a stone miraculously overnight, go for the audition, and get picked from the crowds for my astounding talent. Ha! Dream on, Becca.

"You could play one of the Pink Ladies," said Cat. "Frenchy. You know, the one who goes to beauty school—she has red hair like you."

"Er, she does in the beginning, then she has pink hair, then yellow hair later. Remember the scene where one of the boys says she looks like a beautiful pineapple?"

"Ah, so you *have* been watching it," said Cat.

"Can't avoid it," I said. "I told you, Mac and Squidge are watching it round at Squidge's. That's why I came here, to get away from it. Squidge wants to be one of the T-Birds—you know, John Travolta's sidekick."

"He's called Kenickie," said Cat.

"Mac and I were supposed to be going out, then Squidge talked him into going for a part. I think he wants to be a T-Bird as well."

"He probably wants to because they'd get to wear cool leather jackets, jeans, and shades. But Squidge can't sing for toffee, and I don't think Mac can either."

"Nor can Lia," I said, "but she can dance. I think she's hoping to get into the chorus. And Jade— well, we all know what Jade wants to play."

"The lead," said Cat. "What a joke. Whoever plays Sandy will have to be all wide-eyed and innocent in the first half of the show, and sorry, but I just can't see Jade singing lines like, 'I'm whole-some and pure, oh so scared and unsure.' Er, Jade? No way. You should go for it, Bec. Your voice is just as good as hers."

"I'm not blond like Jade," I said.

"You could wear a wig."

I shook my head. "Nah. I don't think so. Anyway, I'm too fat."

"No way you're fat, you idiot. Oh, come on, Becca, it will be fun. And you have to go public some day.

You can't spend your whole life singing into a hairbrush in front of the mirror or in the shower."

"I sing in our band."

"Yeah, right," said Cat. "And when did we last have a rehearsal? Months ago. Anyway, I don't think Jade wants to be in it anymore. I think she wants to go solo."

"No loss," I said.

Jade is Mac's younger sister and she's in the year above us at our school. At first our band was just me and Cat, then we let Jade join as she has a great voice and we thought it would be good to have three. All the girl bands seem to have three, like Destiny's Child, All Saints, Atomic Kitten . . . but Jade can be a bossy cow and she took over, always telling us what songs we should do and how we should move and what we should wear. The band was called Diamond Heart, but it was turning into Jade and the Diamond Hearts.

Cat switched the video back on.

"Oh no. Please, Cat, let's go out for a bit. It's Sunday. Call Lia and ask her to meet us at Cawsand Beach. Please. You can work on your part later."

In the end, everyone wanted to come. I couldn't believe it when we got to the square down near Cawsand Beach—Lia and Squidge were acting out the dance routine to "You're the One That I Want," with Mac singing the "ooh, ooh, ooh"s in the background. Actually, it was funny, as Squidge and Lia are both completely tone-deaf, and it sounded dreadful. It's a shame that Lia can't sing, because she has the looks to play Sandy—slim, with long blond hair and a beautiful angel face.

A man walked past on the way to the pub and laughed when he heard the singing. "I'd stick to the day jobs if I were you," he called out, putting his fingers in his ears.

"Yeah, give us a break," I said to Lia and Squidge. "You've already frightened the tourists away."

Cat laughed. In the summer, it's heaving with tourists around here, but as the autumn sets in, there's nobody but the locals to be seen.

"The auditions are tomorrow after school," said Squidge, and started jiving with Lia. "And Kenickie doesn't have a solo song, so I've just got to get the moves right and dye my hair back to its normal color."

Squidge's mum, who's a hairdresser, dyed his hair blond at the beginning of term, as he was going through his spiky phase and wanted to look like the guy in *Buffy the Vampire Slayer*.

"Becca, do you think I should dye my hair?" asked Mac, running his hand through his blond hair. "Most of the guys in *Grease* have dark hair."

"It won't matter," I said, beginning to feel left out. "And anyway, we came out here for a break. From now on, this is officially a *Grease*-free zone. Let's do something else, at least for half an hour."

"I can't believe you're not going in for it," said Squidge. "You've easily got the best chance of getting a role, apart from Cat. Isn't there anything we can do to persuade you?"

"Nope," I said, and headed off toward the bay.

"Chicken!" Squidge called after me.

"Sticks and stones, Squidge," I called back. "I've made up my mind."

I turned to look at them as I walked away and noticed that Squidge was whispering something to the others, who all looked at me then nodded. What were they up to? A moment later, they came after me and we all walked down together to the café on the beach. When we got to it, we saw that it was closed for the season, so we went and sat on the wall to watch the boats. There weren't many at this time of year, but it was still good to sit there, watching them bobbing up and down on the waves and breathe in the salty air.

Mac stood behind me and put his arms around me. He felt solid and warm, which was nice, as even though it was bright, there was a chill wind.

"So, Becca . . . ," said Cat, with a sly look at the others.

"What?" I asked, looking at her suspiciously.

"Mates," said Lia. "Mates do things together, don't they?"

"Yeah. Course," I said.

"Together through thick and thin?" asked Squidge.

"Yeah," I said.

"So you wouldn't leave any of us to go through a nerve-wracking experience on our own?" asked Cat.

"No, course not," I said.

"Excellent," she said. "So that means you'll be auditioning with the rest of us tomorrow."

"No way. I told you already. I'm not going up for it."

"Oh, come on," said Lia. "I'm giving it a go and I can't even sing. Please. As mates, moral support. Then we'll all be in it together."

Mac squeezed my shoulders. "Yeah. Come on, Bec. One for all and all for one and all that."

"But . . . ," I began.

"No buts," said Mac. "We think you should go for the part of Sandy. Someone needs to give my sister a run for her money."

"And if I don't?" I asked.

Squidge looked out to the sea then back at the others. "It's *awfully* cold in there at this time of year . . ." He grinned, then nodded at Mac. Mac moved his arms from my shoulders and slipped them under my arms as Squidge picked up my feet. Suddenly, they'd hauled me up between them and were running with me, heading toward the sea.

"If you don't . . ." Mac laughed as they started swinging me over the waves lapping up on to the sand. They were ready to chuck me in!

"*NOOO!!!*" I screamed, half laughing, half panicking. "No. Okay. *Okay*. I'll *do* it."

2

Auditions

"T-BIRDS NEXT," called Miss Segal, sticking her head out into the corridor outside the assembly room. "Then we'll see the Pink Ladies."

A group of boys in fifties gear got up and trooped in after her. They looked great, especially Mac and Squidge who had dressed the part exactly. Both of them had slicked their hair back with gel, turned the collars on their leather jackets up, and looked really cool in their shades. I gave them the thumbs-up.

Most of the school had turned up for the auditions. It was one of the few days in the school calendar when there wasn't a rush for the gate to go home as the bell went at the end of the day. The corridor looked like a scene from Rydell High, the school in the movie. So many people had changed from their school uniform into costumes, and some of the girls were even wearing pink bomber jackets with "The Pink Ladies" sprayed on the back. There was an air of excitement as everyone buzzed about talking about what they were going to sing and who were the favorite contenders for the parts. The lead role of Danny Zucko was bound to go to Jonno Appleton, a complete dish from Year Eleven, and he was strutting up and down making everyone laugh by doing the "Travolta" walk.

For a moment I let myself fantasize about playing the female lead opposite him. It would be brilliant and everyone would be dead jealous. All the girls fancy him; he's cute and tanned, with dark hair and even has a dimple in his chin like John Travolta's. My mum and dad would come to the opening night and clap like crazy whenever I came on, and everyone would admire me for my amazing performance. . . .

I began to wish I'd made more of an effort. I hadn't even thought about dressing for the part and I still wasn't sure which of the songs I was going to do. Still, it should be okay, I thought, as long as Miss Segal didn't want to hear a *whole* song. Last night, I'd learned the opening bars of "Hopelessly Devoted to

You" and the chorus to "Summer Loving," enough to show that I could actually sing in tune (unlike some of the others). What I hadn't realized, though, was that everyone was going to take it so *seriously*. Relax, I told myself as we heard various voices blast out the chorus of the T-Birds' song "Grease Lightning" from the assembly room. I could wing it.

The boys came out a short while later. Mac and Squidge had been told there and then that they didn't have a part, but they both looked quite happy.

"Don't you mind?" I asked Squidge.

"Not at all," he said, grinning. "I didn't really expect to get in, and anyway, Miss Segal asked if I would video the show. Much more my scene."

We call him Squidge because he videos everything and his eye is always squidged up to look through his camera. He wants to be a film director when he's older, so I reckoned Miss Segal had picked the best person in the school to record the show.

"What about you, Mac?" I asked.

"She's asked me to get involved in painting the scenery and stuff," he said.

"Good idea," I said as I watched the next group

of girls, including Cat and Lia, go in to try out for the Pink Ladies parts.

She's smart, this Miss Segal, I thought. She seems to have sussed everyone's talents already and she's only been at the school a short while. It really got me thinking. All my mates are *really* good at something, I realized. Lia's an excellent dancer, Cat's top at singing, Squidge is a really good photographer, and Mac is ace at drawing. But what about me? What do I shine at? I might be okay at a lot of things, but the truth is, I don't stand out at anything.

Then a shiver of anxiety went through me when I realized that the Sandy would be next to be called.

I sat down and mentally went through my lines. It didn't seem long before Cat and Lia came back out to join us in the corridor. Cat looked flushed with excitement and punched the air.

"Got the part?" I asked.

She nodded. "Think so, though it's not official until it's on the notice board tomorrow. And it's pretty definite that Josie Donaghue is going to play

Marty, Kimberley Coleman's playing Jan, and Chloe Barker is Frenchy."

"So that's all the Pink Ladies. What about you, Lia?"

"She said I could be in the chorus." She grinned. "As long as I don't sing too loud. I'm cool with that. I just wanted to be in it."

At that moment, a posse of Sandy lookalikes lined up for their turn to audition. Some had dressed in white nighties with Alice bands in their hair, like Sandy in the sleepover scene where she sings "Hopelessly Devoted," and a couple were in tight PVC pants for the "You're the One That I Want" song at the end. Suddenly I felt hopelessly unprepared, especially when Jade wafted past in a fifties-style gingham dress and looked at my jeans and trainers with disdain. She was just about to say something when we heard Miss Segal calling for the Sandy auditioners.

"Go get 'em, girl," whispered Cat.

Jade was third up, and I have to admit, she was good. She wasn't wearing any makeup, except for a slick of natural lip gloss, and if you didn't know her better, you might have said she passed for innocent. She sang brilliantly, not a word wrong.

Before I knew it, it was my turn and I made my way up on to the stage. As I stood there, I felt very small and wobbly inside, and everyone in the assembly hall turned to watch. The pianist played the opening notes of "Hopelessly Devoted" and I opened my mouth to start, but I missed my timing and the pianist glanced up at me.

"Can I start again?" I asked.

Miss Segal nodded and the pianist started up again.

This time I managed the opening lines and Miss Segal nodded and turned to say something to Mr. Walker, who was sitting next to her.

"Okay, good, Becca, but we just want to hear a bit more," she called. "Can you do the next verse?"

"Um, I'm afraid I only learned the first one," I said as Jade sniggered to one of her mates behind the teachers. "I could do some of 'Summer Living' . . . I mean 'Loving.'"

"Right, off you go," said Miss Segal with a nod at the pianist.

This time I forgot the words after the opening bar. It was like my mind went blank. Everyone was staring. I wanted the ground to open up and swallow me. Miss Segal was looking at me with concern, as though willing me to go on, but I couldn't. The words had gone. My head was empty.

"Okay, you can get down," she said. "Next."

Next up was Dee Hackett, and after her, Susie Richards, but I didn't really take in their performances. I felt mortified. This wasn't anything close to my fantasy. This was my worst nightmare. Of course I wasn't surprised when I wasn't called back at the end with the final three.

I stumbled out into the corridor, made a dash for the door, and ran home.

I read on the notice board the next day that Jade had gotten the part.

3

Parents' Evening

"BECCA, CAN you come down please?" Mum called up the stairs.

Should I pretend to be asleep? I thought as I eyed my duvet. Say I fancied an early night? I looked at my watch. It said eight-thirty. They wouldn't buy it. I took a deep breath and prepared myself to face the inevitable. It wasn't long now until the end of term, and Mum and Dad had just returned from Parents' Evening at our school.

Mum and Dad were waiting for me in the dining room with sheets of paper spread in front of them. Oh *no*, I thought, they've taken *notes*! Parents' evenings can be mad, with so many people milling around, so many teachers to see. I was hoping that they'd have gotten confused and not remembered it all or gotten mixed up about who said what. But no, they'd taken notes.

I tried a smile as I sat down opposite them at the table, but neither of them smiled back. It didn't bode well, so I decided to try Tactic Number Two: Break the ice with a joke.

"So, you must have felt very proud when they all said I'm the school's star pupil. Top in math, top in English, astounding at science . . . er, probably going to be prime minister."

They didn't laugh.

"So," Mum began, "I think we need to talk, Becca."

I decided to try Tactic Number Three: mental retreat and admit to nothing.

"Uh," I said.

Dad looked encouragingly at me. "It's okay, Becca, it wasn't *all* bad."

"So what did they say?"

Mum shook her head. "Well, it's interesting. They all seemed to say the same thing in different ways." She looked at her notes. "Mr. Walker said, 'lacks focus and is a bit of a dreamer.' Mrs. Jeffries said, 'needs to develop staying power if she is to get anything but average.' Mr. Riley said that you need to focus as you could be good at a lot of things, but at the moment, you're more a jack of all trades, master of none. Mr. Nash said you have a good brain and could be a high achiever if only you'd concentrate more." She looked up. "You see what I mean."

I sat on my hands and looked at the carpet. "Er . . ."

"Miss Segal said the same thing. 'Has great potential but unless she knuckles down to some hard work, it's all going to drift by her.'"

There wasn't anything I could say in my defense as I knew I hadn't been working as hard as I could. But, I mean, I'm only fourteen and it's ages before we have to do any important exams.

"Oh," said Dad as he read one of the sheets of paper, "and Miss Segal also said you could have been in the show at the end of term, in the chorus, but you didn't turn up for rehearsals. What was that all about? You told us you didn't get a part."

"I didn't. Not the one I wanted, anyway. I went for the part of Sandy."

I didn't want to tell them how awful it had been. I knew I could have been in the chorus with Lia, but I felt I couldn't join in and pretend I didn't care that

I hadn't got the lead role. I couldn't handle seeing Jade swanning in every day, star of the show, and gloating because I was at the back in the chorus line.

I'd decided to ignore the whole thing and pretend that it hadn't happened. It hadn't been easy, though, as everywhere I went at school, it was *Grease* mania. And all my mates were up to their eyes in it. Cat and Lia were always busy rehearsing. Squidge insisted on videoing behind-the-scenes so that he had a story to tell about the production. And Mac—Mac who I was *supposed* to be going out with—didn't have a moment to spare now that he was painting scenery. I felt like I'd spent most of the term alone.

"Well, young lady . . . ," Mum began.

I winced. I always knew I was going to get a lecture when she called me that. "I think you need to change your attitude. Get down to some serious studying."

"Yes," said Dad. "Show them what you can do, Rebecca. You're a smart girl. Next term we want to see some good grades on your report and none of this dreamer nonsense."

I had to bite my lip. Mum was always berating him for being a dreamer and I almost said, "A dreamer like you then, Dad?" But I knew that it wouldn't have gone down very well, and I didn't want to spark off an argument between them. Lately rows had been getting more and more frequent, always about the same thing. And secretly I was starting to get worried that they might split up like Mac's parents did.

When we had lived in Bristol about four years before, my dad had a proper job in advertising, then he was made redundant. Instead of getting another job, we moved down here where it's cheaper to live, and his plan was to fulfill his lifelong dream of writing a novel. His only sources of income were his savings and an allotment where he grows organic vegetables to supply to Cat's dad's shop. But his savings were running out and that was mainly what the arguing was about. Mum had become the main bread-winner, teaching English to foreign students in Plymouth, and Dad spent his days tapping away at his computer. But so far, he hadn't had any success. He had a file of rejects from agents and publishers, and Mum kept telling him he had to go out and get a "proper" job. Dad kept saying that there weren't any jobs down here in advertising, and anyway, he wasn't ready to give up on being a writer yet. That's when Mum would call him a dreamer. I felt sorry for him in a way, as I knew his writing meant a lot to him.

"Becca, are you listening?" asked Mum.

I nodded. "Yes, work harder. I will. I promise."

I went straight upstairs to commiserate with Cat on the phone.

"They don't understand what it's like," I said.

"I know," said Cat. "I mean, my report was okay except for math. I hate math, and Mr. Riley said I didn't work hard enough at it. I *would* if it was any fun and he'd stop picking on me, but anyway, Dad has been going on and on about it and hasn't said anything about all the good stuff."

"Yeah," I said. "My mum and dad didn't say anything about any of the good stuff either." I didn't tell Cat that I didn't think there *had* been any good stuff.

"It's rotten, isn't it?" said Cat.

"Yeah, rotten. Have you spoken to Lia?"

"Yeah. Hers was okay. She said she reckons the teachers were going easy on her as she's the new girl."

"Maybe. They probably think that if they're too tough on her, she'll want to go back to her old school in London. She only started in September, so I guess they're giving her time to adjust. But she *is* clever. She probably always does well."

"Yeah."

"Yeah," I said. "Ready for tomorrow night?"

"Just about. Bit nervous. In fact I don't think I'll get any sleep tonight, my stomach's in a knot. Tickets are sold out, apparently. Dad's coming, and Jen. Are your mum and dad coming?"

"Nah. They're economizing as usual and weren't bothered about seeing the show as I wasn't in it."

"You could have been."

"Couldn't."

"Could."

"Couldn't, couldn't, couldn't. Okay, 'night Cat. I'm going to call Mac now."

"Hey, have you read about this competition?" he said before I could ask him about Parents' Evening.

"What competition?"

"It's in the paper. Apparently it's going to be nationwide, for all those who felt they missed out on the *Popstars–* and *Pop Idol–* type competitions."

"Oh, not another," I groaned. "There are so many of them now. Every kids' program on telly has a load of hopefuls trying to be the next Britney—*Tot Idol* and all those S Club 7 juniors."

"Yeah," said Mac, "but this new competition is for fourteen- to sixteen-year-olds. The entry age for *Pop Idol* and *Popstars: The Rivals* was over sixteen."

"So what is it this time? Are they looking for a band or just one star?"

"A girl *and* a boy. A Pop Princess and a Pop Prince."

"Oh well, good luck to them," I said. "I don't know why people put themselves through that sort of thing. Some of the judges on that *Pop Idol* program were ruthless. I felt really sorry for some of the contestants. How could they take it?"

"But look at what happens if you win," countered Mac.

"Yeah, but I don't know if it's worth it. Sorry, better go. I need to wish Lia good luck."

"Hi, Lia. You all ready for the opening night tomorrow?"

"Yeah," said Lia. "Sort of. Mum and Dad are coming. And Ollie's coming down from London."

"Really?" Ollie is Lia's divine elder brother. Cat and I both had a crush on him at the beginning of term, but he was more interested in Cat at the time and I decided that "reject" wasn't a role I wanted to play. And then I got together with Mac, so it was all cool in the end. Cat still sees Ollie when he's down from school but doesn't really know where she stands with him. She says she doesn't mind as she just came out of a long relationship with Squidge and doesn't want to get into anything serious just yet, but it's obvious that she really likes him.

"Does Cat know?"

"No. And don't tell her. She's nervous enough as it is and if she knew Ollie was sitting there watching her, I think she'd die. Oh, I hope it all goes okay. I feel so nervous."

Suddenly I felt glad I wasn't in the show. It would be much more enjoyable sitting in the audience watching everybody else sweat.

4

Show Time

I MADE sure I was sitting behind Mr. and Mrs. Axford and Ollie at the show. I wanted to watch Ollie's reaction when Cat was on so that I could tell her about it afterward. I knew she'd want all the details. Everyone was taking sneaky looks at Mr. Axford, otherwise known as Zac Axford, from the famous rock band Hot Snax. With his long hair and leather jacket, he really stood out amid the straight dads dressed in Marks and Spencer's casuals. Mrs. Axford looked fab as usual. She is stunning, with shoulder-length blond hair, and even though the family is dead rich, she always dresses simply, in jeans and a T-shirt. It must be great having parents that cool.

As I sat waiting for the show to start, I felt conspicuous as the only person in school who wasn't involved in the production in some way. There were people from all years rushing about, acting important, ushering, fixing the lights, adjusting loudspeakers, selling programs. The hall was packed with parents and friends, and there was an excited buzz in the audience as the lights went down and the music to "Love Is a Many Splendored Thing" struck up off stage. The curtain rose and there were Jade and Jonno, going into the first number on a beach set painted by Mac. After that we were transported to Rydell High, and I had to stop myself standing up and applauding when Cat came on as Rizzo. Ollie looked well impressed; in fact everyone looked impressed when she started to sing. I felt a twinge of jealousy, just for a moment. I wished I'd worked harder to get a part; then everyone would be watching me with the same admiration. The feeling didn't last long, though, as I knew in private that it was my own fault that I didn't have a part.

As the show got going, I was pulled in and really began to enjoy it. Apart from one scene when Kimberley Coleman got her dance steps mixed up, it went without a hitch, and at the end the audience gave them a standing ovation. It was only then that Cat caught sight of Ollie, who was standing, cheering with the rest of them. She looked shocked for a minute, and I was glad she hadn't seen him before as he might have put her off. But he gave her the thumbs-up and she grinned back at him.

After the curtain had gone down and people got up to leave, I went backstage. Of course Squidge was there filming away, and Mac was busy carrying out bits of scenery.

"Brilliant, weren't they?" said Mac.

I nodded. "And so was your scenery. It looked great."

"Thanks."

"And Cat and Lia were fab."

"They were, weren't they?" said Mac. "In fact, having seen her tonight, I'm going to tell Cat she should go in for that competition—you know, for Pop Princess. She's easily good enough. Jade's been on about it for days. Course she's already got plans to enter, but I think Cat should as well. She was great tonight. I reckon she could win."

I waited for him to suggest that I go in for it as well, but the thought didn't seem to have occurred to him, and for a moment I felt miffed.

Why didn't he think that I'd stand a chance?

"Hey, Becca," called Cat as she came out of the dressing room with the other girls.

I gave her a big hug. "Well done! I was so proud of you." Then I caught sight of Ollie coming toward us with a bunch of freesias. "And I don't think I was the only one."

Cat blushed when she saw Ollie, so I decided to make myself scarce for a moment and went to find Lia. I popped my head around the dressing-room door and there was Jade, surrounded by her mates. She caught my eye and gave me one of her "What are you doing here?" looks, but I decided to be generous. She *had* been good, after all, and I would be friends with her if she would just be a bit nicer.

"Fab show, Jade," I said. "Well done—you were really top."

She looked like she was going to faint with shock. "Oh, right, thanks," she stuttered.

I laughed to myself. I may have felt a bit jealous, but I believe in giving credit where it's due.

"Thank God that's over." Lia laughed, coming up

from behind me with Squidge in tow. "Now we can all relax."

"No," said Squidge. "I think we should move on. Today Torpoint, tomorrow the world."

"What are you on about, Squidge?" I asked.

"We have to think big," he said. "So Becca, truth, dare, kiss, or promise?"

"What, *now*?" I asked.

"Yeah. *Now*. Come on. Quick."

"Okay. Dare," I said.

"Good," said Squidge. "I was hoping you'd pick that one."

"Lia, truth, dare, kiss, or promise?"

"Promise," she said.

He called over to Cat, who was deep in conversation with Ollie. "Truth, dare, kiss, or promise?" he asked.

She looked flirtily at Ollie. "Dare." She smiled up at him.

"Excellent." Squidge grinned as he pulled a piece of newspaper out of his back pocket. "I have *un grando* dare for Becca and Cat. You know this competition for Pop Prince and Pop Princess? Well, I

dare both of you"—he looked pointedly at me—
"and I mean, *both* of you, to go up for it. Lia, you
picked promise, so you have to promise to go as
well. Mac and I have already decided to give it a go.
Auditions are in Plymouth next Saturday."

5 You Got to Have a Dream

MUM BROUGHT the post in and put one of the envelopes in front of Dad.

"What's that?" He looked up, smiling, from his breakfast of toast and Marmite. "Not another rejection, I hope."

"No," said Mum.

He scanned the letter. "Oh."

"Yes," said Mum. "The building insurance renewal. Three hundred and eighty pounds and it's due by the end of the month."

I started to get up to go. I didn't want to witness another of their rows.

"We'll find a way," said Dad.

Mum folded her arms in front of her. "You mean *I'll* find a way. Where are you going to get that kind of money?"

As I was leaving, Dad glanced up at me with

concern, then focused on his toast. I felt really sorry for him. He looked so helpless when she started on at him.

I crept upstairs to my bedroom and got out the newspaper cutting that Squidge had given me the night before.

Are you the next best thing? it said. *Rocket Productions are looking for a new Pop Prince and Pop Princess. Auditions in Plymouth Town Hall on Saturday 14th and Sunday 15th December, 9 a.m. to 8 p.m. Come prepared with a song of your choice. Entry age: 14–16 years. Prize £5,000 each for our Prince and Princess, and a recording deal to make a single.*

I leaned back and closed my eyes. First I imagined myself handing the check over to Mum and Dad. That should stop them rowing. All the press would want to know me, I'd be given a top make-over, my photo would be on the front of all the magazines. Everyone at school would be so jealous when my single went straight to number one. I'd win an award at the Grammys; in fact I'd present an award with my new best friend Kylie Minogue. I'd be a stone thinner and wearing an amazing sparkly designer dress and shoes, my hair would be perfectly straight for a change, and afterward I'd go to an all-celebrity party with Robbie and Eminem and Madonna. Ohmigod, I thought as I folded the paper away, here I go again. The teachers were right—I *am* a dreamer.

At that moment, Dad stuck his head round the door. "You in there, Bec?" he said, then came in and sat at the end of my bed. "What you up to?"

I showed him the newspaper cutting. "We thought we might go in for it."

Dad read the cutting. "Who's we?"

"Me, Lia, Cat, Mac, and Squidge. Squidge dared me. Squidge, Mac, and Lia know that they won't really stand a chance because they can't sing, but Mac says it will be a laugh. Squidge wants to do it for experience, he said. You know what he's like, always going on about how a film director needs to have lots of different experiences in life."

Dad laughed. "And you and Cat? Reckon you're in with a chance?"

I shrugged. "Dunno. . . . Dad, do you think I'm a dreamer?"

"Well, your report—," he began.

"But what I mean is, is it a bad thing to be?"

Dad looked at me closely. "Yes and no. Yes, if it's affecting your schoolwork. It does help to know where you're going and to focus. But otherwise, no. Everything has its good and bad side, and the other side to being a dreamer is having an imagination and that's an excellent thing. No, I think you have to have a dream and you have to follow that dream."

"Your dream is to get your novel published, isn't it?"

Dad nodded. "It is, but it can take years to become successful. I'm not going to give up."

"Even though . . ."

"Even though," said Dad, then patted my hand. "Things aren't so bad, Becca. I've still got some savings left, and I'm not going to let you or your mum down. Don't you worry. And one day, my work will land on the right desk. The main thing is you have to believe in yourself, even when it seems like nobody else does."

"You mean Mum?"

"Mum believes in me in her own way. It's just . . . sometimes she doesn't show it. I know she worries when the bills come in . . . but enough about me. Let's talk about you. This competition. I think it's a great idea you go up for it. Squidge is right about having experiences, and not only if you want to be a film director. But you mustn't be disappointed if you don't get through. You mustn't take it personally. When I get those rejections from the publishers, of course I feel disappointed for a day or so, then I put the letter in the file with the others and send my stuff off to the next one. Success is fifty percent talent and fifty percent perseverance."

"So I can go in for it?"

"Of course you can. In fact I'll drive you over." He grinned, then he began to sing, "'You got to have a dream. If you don't have a dream, how you gonna have a dream come true?'"

I gave him a hug. "I believe in your dream, Dad."

Cat and Lia came over later in the afternoon to do some homework for social science. The week before we'd had a lecture from a visiting social worker who'd given us a lesson in political correctness and we were supposed to think of some terms that could be seen as offensive to some people and think of another way of phrasing it.

"This is too boring," I said, putting down my pen. "I can't think of anything. Why don't we go through my CD collection and decide what songs we'll do at the audition?"

I spread all my CDs on the floor and we sat down and began to sift through.

"I got Whitney, Mariah Carey, Janet Jackson, Atomic Kitten, Destiny's Child, All Saint's, Kylie . . ."

"Actually, I think I'd like to do 'Hero,' by Mariah Carey," said Cat. "I listened to it this morning and wrote out all the words."

Lia picked up a Britney Spears CD. "Maybe I could do 'Baby One More Time.'"

"Good idea," I said.

"What about you, Bec?" asked Lia.

"Not sure yet," I said, looking at the CDs. "Maybe 'Crazy For You,' by Madonna, or maybe an Anastacia number. Dunno."

"How long do we actually get to perform?" asked Lia.

"Oh, only a couple of minutes, if that," I said. "They'll either like you or not."

"They'll be able to tell with me in the first ten seconds."

I looked at Lia with admiration. If I couldn't sing, you wouldn't catch me anywhere near the competition. She must be very secure, I thought, like she doesn't feel she has to prove anything. Then a thought flashed through my mind. So what am I trying to prove?

"I think you're amazing, Lia," I said. "Putting yourself up for this."

"Not really," she said. "I mean, I know I don't stand a chance so I don't have any expectations—it'll be fun. But it will be harder for you and Cat because you do stand a chance."

"I know. I'm feeling nervous already," I said.

"You'll be great," said Cat. "You look good."

"No, I don't!" I interrupted. "I need to lose a ton of weight."

Cat sighed. "You're blind, Becca. You look perfect

and you sing well. You should do a ballad, something to really show off your voice."

She's such a good mate, Cat. We're going to be competing against each other and yet, here she is, being really encouraging. She's so supportive of her friends. Jade, on the other hand, has apparently been practicing in secret for weeks. Mac told us that she knew about the competition before any of us and didn't mention it to anyone. He said that she's really miffed that we're all going in for it as she thought it was her special thing. What cheek. The competition's open to anyone.

"Most important, though," said Lia, "is what are we going to wear?"

"Yeah, course," I said. "There might be some decent boys there."

"*Becca,*" said Cat. "You have a boyfriend, remember? Mac?"

I grinned. "No harm in looking."

"Oh, don't say you've gone off him already," said Cat.

"What do you mean?"

"Well, you know what you're like."

"No, I don't know what I'm like. Tell me."

The atmosphere in the room suddenly felt tense and I sensed I was being got at.

Cat looked at me anxiously. "You know, with boys . . ."

"What are you saying, Cat?"

"Um, nothing . . . not really, just, er, well . . . okay, what you *were* like before you met Mac. Always changing your mind, in love with a different boy each week."

"I *never* was."

"Okay, what about Laurence Grant, Robin Barker, Phil . . . Ollie . . ."

I suddenly saw the funny side. "D'oh. Oh yeah— Mark Jones, Dave McIntosh . . . yeah, I suppose, but I never did anything with any of them. I never got off with them or anything. It was only in my head . . . oh no!"

"What?" said Lia.

"In my *head*." I looked at both of them. "Do you think I'm a dreamer? You know, like always fantasizing and never doing anything about it?"

Cat gave me a hug. "That's why we like you, Becca. You make life interesting with all your dreams and ideas. But you're not going to mess Mac around, are you?"

I shook my head. "Nah, no, course not, but it's not as though we're married or anything. I mean, we're having a nice time and that, but it's not like, well, what you and Squidge were like, Cat. I mean, you went out with him for years."

"Yeah, like an old married couple we were," said Cat, then she laughed. "So what you're saying is, it's not that you're not into commitment, but rather you are monogamously challenged."

I laughed. "Yeah, that's brilliant," I said, getting my homework out again. "*Now* I get what the social worker was on about. And I got one." I put on my best snotty voice. "One mustn't say, 'stop nagging;' one ought to say, 'stop being verbally repetitive,' as it is less offensive."

We all got our books out again and for the next ten minutes, there was no stopping us.

Lia giggled. "You mustn't say 'drunk;' you must say 'chemically inconvenienced,'" she said. "And you can't say 'male chauvinist pig;' you have to say 'a man with swine empathy.'"

Cat cracked up. "Okay, here's some of mine. You

43

can't say someone's a tart; rather you should say she's sexually focused. You can't say someone has big boobs; rather she is pectorally superior. Becca, you got any more?"

I nodded. "Someone isn't bald; he's in follicle regression. A woman doesn't have a big tummy; she has developed a chocolate storage facility."

"Excellent," said Lia, putting her books away. "That should keep old Jeffries happy. Now back to more important things. What are we going to wear to Plymouth—glitzy or casual?"

I felt relieved. The atmosphere was light again.

Cat considered the question. "Hmmm . . . I don't think we should dress up too much; it might look like we trying too hard."

"And all the serious performers always turn up for auditions in working clothes," said Lia, "like leggings, torn T-shirts, and scuffed trainers, to show that what's important to them is their art."

"Oh yes, my art . . ." I laughed. "Oh, luvvie darlings, tear me a T-shirt, will you? Then run out and get me an Evian. Evian mind, not Perrier, or any other brand. I *must* have my Evian."

Pop Idol

6

"LOOK WHAT I got," said Mac, waving a video at us when we arrived at Squidge's the next Friday after school. "I nicked it from Jade's room when she wasn't looking."

It was the *Raw Talent* video, a compilation of the *Pop Idol* episodes that were on telly.

"Brilliant," said Cat, following Squidge into his living room. "Put it on."

Wow, Jade's really been doing her homework, I thought as Mac put the video in the player and we settled down to watch. Hah, just you wait Jade Macey, because this time *I've* been practicing too. I'd decided to do "Not That Kind," by Anastacia and had gone over and over it until it was perfect. I wasn't going to let Saturday be a repeat of the *Grease* audition where I dried up. This time I'd be ready.

As the video started and we watched the crowds waiting to go in for their auditions, I felt a surge of excitement go through me. Tomorrow it would be us out there among the hopefuls.

"Ohmigod," said Lia as the video progressed to showing the actual auditions. "Are we really going to put ourselves through this?"

"We are," said Mac, but he was starting to look a bit worried as well as we watched one of the judges tear to shreds yet another contestant's performance.

Squidge noticed and punched his arm. "You're not going to bottle out now, are you, mate?"

"Um, no," said Mac. "Course not."

Suddenly my heart sank. Someone on screen was singing "Not That Kind."

"But that's my song," I said.

Not long later, another contestant sang Britney's "Baby One More Time."

"That's *my* song," said Lia.

Then someone did "Hero" and Cat cried, "And that's my song!"

"You sound like the three bears out of 'Goldilocks and the Three Bears,'" said Mac, laughing. "And the little bear said, 'and that's *my* porridge.'"

As the video progressed, it got worse. A whole

load of people did songs by Anastacia and one of the judges actually said that if anyone else did one by her, he would hit them.

"No wonder Jade didn't want to share this," said Lia. "She asked me on Monday what songs we were doing, but when I told her, she didn't say anything."

Cat put her head in her hands. "We've got to pick new songs, guys. Songs that haven't been done to death on *Pop Idol*."

"Oh no. How?" I said, looking at my watch. "The competition's tomorrow."

"Chill, you guys," said Squidge. "I don't reckon it matters. Whatever you choose, there's bound to be someone else doing it as well. It's whether you can impress the judges or not that counts. Want to see what I'm doing?"

I nodded and Squidge got up and went into an ear shattering, rocked up version of the Talking Heads number "Psycho Killer." What he lacked in vocals, he certainly made up for in enthusiasm and the rest of us split our sides laughing.

"I'm going to wear one of my dad's suits," said

Squidge, "like David Byrne from the Talking Heads. What do you think?"

"Different," said Cat.

"Don't give up the day job," I said.

Squidge smiled. "I won't. But look, it's going to be a laugh, an *experience*. If we take it seriously, then we won't enjoy it."

"Right," I said. But I was beginning to have doubts. The judges on *Pop Idol* had been ruthless in their criticisms and some of the contestants were in tears afterward. And suddenly I didn't feel so confident about *anything*—my hair, my weight, or my choice of song.

"At least this video has given us an idea of what to expect," I ventured.

"Yeah," said Mac. "Assassination."

"Yeah," sighed Lia. "But at least you and Cat can sing."

"That doesn't seem to make much difference," said Cat. "Even some of the good ones got thrown out because the judge didn't like their face or clothes or something. I think Squidge is right. We go for a laugh—no expectations. That way there'll be no disappointments."

"Right," said Lia. "So what are you going to do, Mac?"

He started tugging at the fly on his jeans. "I got something to show you."

"*Mac,*" said Cat as Mac started taking off his jeans, "*what* are you doing?"

Mac stripped off to his boxers, then he turned round and bent over. On the back of his boxers, he'd written, "Vote for Mac."

We all cracked up.

"Are you honestly going to do that?" I said.

Mac nodded. "Well, I know my voice isn't memorable, but my boxers will be."

"But what song are you going to do?" asked Cat.

"'Hang the DJ,' by the Smiths."

"Don't know that one," I said.

"The song's actually called 'Panic,' but the chorus goes, 'Hang the DJ, hang the DJ, hang the DJ . . . ,'" said Mac.

"But are you *sure* you want to do a song with those words? What if one of the judges is a DJ?"

Mac grinned. "Then I'll have the sympathy of the contestants."

"I think it's brilliant," said Squidge.

"But what are *we* going to do now?" I asked, looking at Cat and Lia. "Maybe I shouldn't go."

"Oh, come on, Becca, don't back out now," said Squidge.

"But I don't know what to do now that I've seen that video. I spent *ages* practicing my Anastacia song. But having seen what that judge said about wanting to hit the next person who sang one, I'll have to do something more original."

"Not necessarily," said Mac. "They'll be different judges tomorrow, won't they?"

"God, I hope so," said Cat. "I don't think I could face that panel from *Pop Idol*."

"Why learn a new song, Cat?" asked Squidge. "Why don't you do Rizzo's song from *Grease*? It showed off your voice. You know it inside out, so if you get nervous, you probably won't forget the lines."

Lia and I nodded.

Cat beamed. "Good idea. You're right. I do know the words backward, and if I do it, I won't have to stay up half the night learning a new one. In fact, Lia, why don't you do one of the songs from *Grease*? Saves you all the hassle of learning something new as well."

"Yeah and I could do the dance steps we learned

at school. That way, I can at least show them that I can do *something*."

"So that leaves you, Becca," said Squidge. "Fancy another go at 'Hopelessly Devoted'?"

"My version didn't include the devoted part," I said. "It was just hopeless. So no way. Once was more than enough. No . . . oh God, so what am I going to do?" I cast my mind over all the songs we'd done in our band. None of them seemed right for a solo. "The only other song I know all the way through is 'You've Got a Friend,' by Carole King. I know it off by heart because my mum always plays it in the car whenever we go anywhere."

"So let's hear it," said Cat.

I stood up and took a deep breath. I felt really nervous. This is mad, I thought. I have to do it, but if I feel this bad with my mates, how on Earth am I going to feel at the audition? Come on, Becca, I told myself. You can do it, and it's only for a laugh. I took another breath, then launched into the song.

After I'd finished, I took a quick look at the others. They all had wide grins on their faces.

"You're really good, Becca," said Cat. "And your voice suits that song. I think you're in with a real chance, even more than if you did the Anastacia one."

"Really?" I asked.

Mac nodded. "Definitely. In fact I can just see you going up to get your Golden Globe Award. The cameras will be flashing. You'll be in an off-the-shoulder Versace number, looking fab. I'll be somewhere in the crowd, trying to get your attention—'Becca, Becca, remember me? I knew you when you were nobody. Spare a moment for an old friend?'"

I laughed. "No way, José. You'll be on my *arm*, my escort. And Cat will be going up to receive her award, just in front of me with Squidge and Lia."

Maybe it was okay to have mad fantasies, I thought, as long as you didn't take them too seriously.

Round One

7

DAD DROPPED Lia, Cat, and me off outside the hall in Plymouth, where already there was a long queue waiting for the doors to open.

"Knock 'em dead," said Dad as we got out of the car. "I'll go and do some jobs in town, so ring me on your mobile when you're ready to be picked up later this afternoon."

"Right, Dad," I said as I scanned the queue. There were all sorts there—cute, glam, hippie, small, tall, fat, skinny . . . some with their parents, a few boys with dreadlocks, a girl with pink hair, one with a shaven head and loads of earrings, lots of girls in tiny tops showing pierced navels even though the weather was freezing. Cat, Lia, and I had come well prepared for a long wait in the cold, with jackets, scarves, and gloves. I'd worn my black jeans, a black halter top underneath my jacket, and a black baseball cap that Dad had bought me with the word "Princess" written on it in sequins. Lia had on her baggy jeans, a tiny top, and a Mulberry handkerchief on her head. Cat was in faded jeans and an off-the-shoulder top. The boys had arrived already. Squidge looked like a star in his dad's suit and tie with black shades, and Mac wore his jeans and flash Adidas trainers. I thought we looked pretty cool, not mad like some of the others.

"Fab cap," said one of the girls as we joined the queue. "I should have thought of that."

"Thanks," I said as I watched a tall black girl in front begin to do stretching exercises.

"Shall we make a run for it now or later?" asked Lia as a couple of girls in front burst into song and were absolutely pitch perfect.

"Later," I said. Even though the size of the crowd was daunting, I felt excited, and now that we were there, I wanted to be part of it. It was hysterical— Squidge had brought his video to film everything and because he looked like an executive in his suit, everyone thought he was from the telly. Some girls were flirting openly with him and singing their songs for him. I guess they were hoping that they'd be put in a program showing edited highlights later. Little did they know that they probably would, but the video would only be seen by an audience of five teenagers.

The doors opened at nine on the dot, and the line slowly moved through the entrance. When we got inside, there were a number of people at tables taking our details as we filed past, then each of us was given a sticky label. The boys' labels had "Pop Prince" written on them with a number, and the girls' had "Pop Princess" and a number.

"Hi, I'm Tanya," said a lady with red spiky hair when we reached the registration tables. "Put the label on your top so that we can see it, and go into the hall down the corridor, on the right, then wait until your number is called."

Once inside the hall, I forgot my nerves as there were so many people to look at. But then I caught sight of Jade and a couple of her mates from Year Ten and my heart sank.

"Oh *no*," I said. "Jade's got a cap on exactly like

mine and she'll go in before me. Pants."

"Stick your label over the sequined princess on your cap," Cat suggested. "Then it won't look the same, and yours will say 'Pop Princess' not just 'Princess.'"

"Good idea," I said and took the label off my top. Loads of other people had done similar things. Some had stuck their labels on their trousers or on their abdomens and one guy had even stuck his on his forehead.

As we settled ourselves in a corner on the floor, Tanya came in and called for the first fifty to go and wait in a corridor outside the audition room.

"We're in for a long wait," said Mac, pointing at his number. He was number 223, Squidge was 224, Cat was 225, Lia was 226 and I was 227. "Did anyone bring anything to eat?"

I shook my head. I hadn't even thought about food and suddenly I realized that I was starving. All around us people were eating sandwiches and crisps and my stomach started gurgling.

"Ohmigod," I said. "If I can't remember the words of my song, my stomach will sing it for me."

I quickly forgot about my hunger when the hall started buzzing as the first person came out of the audition. He was followed by another then another, then another. News of the judges spread through the hall like a Mexican wave.

"There's three judges," said Cat, after she'd eavesdropped on a couple of boys by a radiator. "Two blokes and one woman."

"And one of them is a DJ from a London radio station," said Mac, coming back in from the loo. "Eek. He's gonna love my song."

I was beginning to get butterflies as we continued to wait. A few people came back in, or rather leaped in, telling people that they'd got through. Others looked downcast and disappointed and came back shaking their heads, or in tears.

"Oh God," I said to Cat. "People are crying already. I can feel my stomach tightening into a knot. I'm so nervous."

"I know," said Cat. "And I have to go to the loo *again*."

"We'll come with you," Lia and I chorused.

As we set off for the loo for the third time that

morning, it was amazing to witness all the mini-dramas unfolding in the corridors. One girl was weeping on her mum's shoulder, another guy was mouthing off about one of the judges, loads of people were doing warm-up exercises, some were practicing their songs. Even in the loos, girls were leaning on the sinks and singing into the mirrors.

On our way back to the hall, I noticed Jade dancing about with a mate.

"Looks like Jade's through," I said to Lia.

"I thought she would be," Lia replied. "She may be a top bitch, but she can sing."

Eleven o'clock went by, twelve o'clock, one o'clock . . . then, thank God, a couple of lads appeared and set up a table selling sandwiches and juices. As we lined up to buy something, we started chatting with some of the other contestants, and it became apparent that some of them were taking it deadly seriously. There was a group from a drama school in Bristol and they clearly saw the competition as their big chance to break into show business.

"There's some real talent here," said Cat as one girl in the line rehearsed "Killing Me Softly."

"I know," I said. "Some of them are . . . like, really professional. I was chatting to one girl over there, and she's been singing since she was five, in shows and stuff."

"And everyone's talking about the *Pop Idol* and *Rivals* programs," said Mac, "and wondering if one of the judges is going to be nasty."

"Bound to be," said Squidge. "If they film any of this, it makes better telly if there's a bad guy and some tears. Then you get everyone reacting to him and what he says. That judge in *Pop Idol* is probably a nice bloke, really, but that was the part he had to play."

"Do you think?" I asked. "I thought he was just plain horrible and so insulting sometimes. He destroyed some contestants."

"It all makes good telly," said Squidge. "And see? It worked. It got everyone talking about the show."

"I guess," I said, but I hoped there wouldn't be a judge like that on our panel.

Midafternoon, Tanya came back in. "Two hundred to two hundred and fifty," she called. "If you could go and wait in the corridor."

"*Aargghhh*, that's us," said Lia. "Whose stupid idea was this anyway? What am I doing here? I must be mad."

"You'll be fine," I said. "And you look great." Secretly, though, I felt the same—I must be insane to put myself through this.

Even Squidge looked a bit nervous. "It's a laugh, it's a laugh, it's a laugh," he chanted as we trooped out with the others.

Once in the corridor, we sat down on the chairs lining the walls and waited.

"I'm not being bitchy," whispered Cat as a skinny-looking boy with round shoulders and bad spots got up to go into the audition room, "but you can tell just by looking at some people that they're not going to get through."

"I know," I said. "Poor guy. He looks terrified."

"Well, good on him for trying," said Squidge. "But in the end, I guess they're going to want a Pop Prince or Princess to look the part as well as be able to sing."

"That's me out as well, then," I said.

Squidge punched my arm. "Do you have one of

those fairground mirrors at home—the ones that distort your image? Because you just don't see it, do you? You look fab!"

I didn't feel fab, but it was nice to hear it anyway.

Along with the others waiting in the corridor, we strained to hear the skinny boy's performance. He was completely flat and came out only moments later, shaking his head.

"How was it?" Lia asked as he walked past us.

"Nightmare," he said. "They said it was the worst audition they'd ever heard."

Lia smiled at him. "Ah well, they haven't heard me yet, have they?"

Some went in and sounded fantastic, and others were like the skinny boy and sounded awful. One girl came out in floods of tears.

"I couldn't remember the words," she sobbed. "It was awful with all them sitting there staring at me."

"That happened to me once," I said. "You'll get another chance some other time."

"Do you think?" she said hopefully.

"Sure," I said.

Then we got chatting to a guy who looked like a real laugh. He was wearing a grass skirt and a Hawaiian shirt.

"I can't sing," he said, "so I'm going to do an instrumental version of the theme to *Hawaii Five-O*."

"Can I film you?" asked Squidge.

"Yeah," he said, and went into his routine, complete with Hawaiian dancing. "Da da da da daaah da, da da da da da."

We all fell about laughing, and Tanya came out and told Squidge to put away his camera, then told the rest of us to "pipe down." Hawaiian boy made faces behind her back and it was good to know that there was at least one person there who wasn't treating the situation like it was life or death.

Tanya reappeared moments later and looked up and down the corridor.

"Two hundred and twenty-three," she called.

"Oh God, that's me," said Mac. He went white and stood up, looking as though he was going off to see the dentist for some very nasty root work. After the door closed behind him, we all shot over to the door and strained to hear. We heard him say something, then could just about make out the words "Hang the DJ." He was back out in a flash.

"Phew," he said. "Don't remind me to do that again in a hurry."

"Two hundred and twenty-four," called Tanya, and Squidge got up to go in.

"How was it?" I asked as Mac slumped down on the floor next to us.

"They just look at you," he said. "No expression. No nothing."

"What did they say?" asked Lia.

"They asked why I saw myself as the next Pop Prince."

"What did you say?" I asked.

He grinned. "Because I have blue blood. They didn't laugh, though. Then the woman said, 'Do you realize that you can't sing?'"

"What did you say?" I asked.

"I said yes, but that one ought to be positive in life," said Mac. "Then they did smile, and one of the blokes said, 'Well sorry, mate, this isn't your competition and we won't be asking you to London.'"

"You should have said that saying you can't

sing is offensive," I said. "'Vocally challenged' would be much more sensitive."

"Did you show them your boxers?" asked Cat.

Mac shook his head. "Nah, bottled out. You'll see what it's like when you get in there. I couldn't do it."

Squidge came out a moment later. He was grinning from ear to ear.

"Two hundred and twenty-five," called Tanya, and Cat got up to go.

"Eep," she said.

"You'll be fine," I said, squeezing her arm as she went past. "Remember to breathe."

"Oh yeah," said Cat and took a deep breath.

"Are you in?" I asked Squidge as Cat disappeared behind the door.

"Nah," he said. "But they said I may have a good career ahead of me, frightening young children."

As he reached into his rucksack to get his camera, I stuck my ear to the door to hear Cat. She was singing the opening bars of Rizzo's number and sounded really good, confident. Then it went quiet then I could hear them talking. Oh, please don't let them say anything horrible to her, I prayed.

She came out a moment later with Tanya.

"Two hundred and twenty-six," said Tanya as Cat grinned at me from behind her and gave me the thumbs-up.

"You're in?" I whispered to Cat as Lia got up to go with Tanya.

She nodded, still grinning. "Yeah," she said. "Good luck, Lia."

Poor Lia. She sang "Summer Loving," but stopped after a few lines. Then all we could hear was the murmur of voices.

She was back out a moment later, shaking her head. She didn't look too freaked, though, just relieved that it was over.

"Two hundred and twenty-seven," called Tanya.

"You're on, kid," said Squidge as he pointed his camera at me.

Oh God, I thought as I followed Tanya into the room. This is it.

The room was smaller than I expected, like a conference room in a hotel. The three judges were sitting at one end, behind a table with glasses and bottles of water on it. The woman looked in her thirties—pretty, with short dark hair. One of the men was plump and looked older, maybe as old as fifty—balding, with mousy hair. The other man was dark, with glasses, and good-looking in a Tom Cruise kind of way. They were talking among themselves and one of them said something that made the other two laugh. I stood at the door, wondering what to do. My hands were sweating and I felt numb, like time was standing still.

The woman finally looked over at me and gave me a friendly smile. "Well, come in," she said, pointing to the floor about six feet away from their table, "and stand on the circle."

In the middle of the floor, there was a white circle, so I walked over to it and stood there, trying to stop my knees from shaking.

"Shall I begin?" I asked.

"First, tell us your name," said the older man.

"Becca Howard," I said.

"Where are you from?"

"St. Antony, Cornwall."

"Ah, come with your mates, have you?" said the

woman, looking at her notes. "The last four?"

I nodded.

"Age?"

"Fourteen."

"And why do you think you might be our Pop Princess, Becca?"

The words "Because it's my dream" were out before I could think about it.

"Okay, then, away you go," said the woman.

Imagine you're in the car with Mum, I thought as I took a deep breath and started: "'When you're down and troubled . . .'"

Halfway through the song, the older man held up his hand. "Okay, that's enough." He then turned to his companions and said something.

Prepare to die, I told myself as all the awful things the judges had said to the contestants on *Pop Idol* flashed through my mind—"You're no singer," "You think you're a Ferrari when actually you're a Skoda," "You're an insult to the song" . . .

"Okay, I'll start," said the woman to the other two judges. "Yeah, good. I think you were a bit nervous in the beginning, but that's understandable. But you got going and your voice has a nice throaty quality. So, yes. A yes from me. Martin, what did you think?"

The older man looked me up and down and nodded. "Hmmm," he said. "Not sure. We're looking for star quality here. The X-factor, something that hits you the minute the person walks through the door. Not sure that's you, Becca. You looked more like a timid mouse when you first came in, not a confident pop star, so I'm afraid it's a no from me.' He turned to the last judge. "Looks like you have the deciding vote, Paul."

"I think it was a good choice of song for your voice," he said, "and I think you did it justice. We're looking for genuine talent here and no doubt, you can sing. Confidence? Well, that can always be worked on so, yes, I'd like to give you another chance."

I think I felt my jaw drop, and I stood there for a minute gawping at them.

"Okay then, out-voted," said Martin, with a grin at me. "So, you can go now, Becca, and you're through to the next round."

I wanted to rush forward and hug them all. "Thank you, thanks, thank you . . ."

I stumbled out into the corridor where the rest of the gang were waiting expectantly.

"I'm *through*!" I cried. "I can't *believe* it. I'm through and they were so nice."

Cat gave me a huge hug and we jumped up and down on the spot. Then Mac, Squidge, and Lia put their arms around us and we jumped about in a circle.

"Knew you would be," said Mac.

"Arghhh," said Cat.

"I know!" I replied. *"Arrrghhhhhhh."*

8

Roller-Coaster Ride

MR. WALKER, our English teacher at school, says that life is a roller coaster—up, down, and round and round we go. I sat in my bedroom thinking about it later that day. Down I'd gone with the audition at school for Sandra Dee in *Grease*, then up, up, up, I'd gone today in Plymouth. It was one of the best feelings in the world to be picked. I'd remember it forever. I was through to the next round! Only a hundred people were chosen from four cities to go up to London the following Saturday and I was one of them. It had been totally top. Cat was over the moon too, and Lia also got her moment, even though she wasn't through for the next audition. The telly crew had turned up in the corridor when I was auditioning and made a beeline for her. They interviewed her for the program they're doing on the competition, then filmed all of us jumping up and down when I came out after my go.

Dad was thrilled when he came to pick us up, genuinely chuffed. But then we got home and I told Mum.

"No," she said, and turned away to put the kettle on.

"But, *Mum*," I pleaded, "this is the chance of a lifetime. I *can't* not go."

Mum turned back and looked uncomfortable. "Look, Becca, don't get me wrong. I'm really happy that you had a good time today. . . ."

"It wasn't exactly a good time," I objected. "Well, it *was* in the end—it was brilliant—but God, if you'd been there when we were all waiting . . . it was *nerve*-wracking. Much worse than waiting for exam results."

"I know," said Dad. "It took a lot of guts to do what you did today. I'm really proud of you."

"So why can't I go to London, then?"

Mum sighed. "A number of reasons, Becca. One: This wanting to be a pop star has just come out of the blue—"

"No, it hasn't. You *know* it hasn't. I've always

wanted to sing. What about my band with Cat—Diamond Heart?"

"You abandoned that weeks ago. And you know what you're like, Becca. In the summer you wanted to be a vet, last month it was an air hostess, before that a TV presenter. If I thought you were serious about any of it, you know you'd have my full support."

"But I *am* serious about this. I really am. You *have* to believe me. Before I didn't know what I wanted to do and that's why I could never make up my mind. But I know now. Oh please, Mum, I have to go."

"Chances like this don't come round often, Meg," said Dad. "A great experience, even if nothing comes of it."

Mum got up from the table and started stacking dishes irritably, then she turned to us. "It's not fair. Why do *I* have to be the bad guy in all of this? Always the one who says no. Honestly, Joe, you know the real reason."

"What?" I asked.

Mum looked at Dad. "London!" she said. "And where do you think she's going to stay? How do you think she's going to get there? These kinds of trips cost money, never mind some kind of chaperone. I can't take time off and you can't go, Joe."

"But it's at the weekend." I looked pleadingly at Dad, but he had his defeated look on. Money. Same old story. He didn't have a leg to stand on.

"You'd have to go up on the Friday. You'd need money for travel," said Mum wearily. "Money for a place to stay. Money for food."

Oh, not this again, I thought. How I wished I'd done a paper round, like Squidge and Cat did. Then I could have saved some of my own money. Maybe it wasn't too late.

"I'll get a job," I said.

"Be practical, Becca," said Mum. "London's next Saturday. I don't think any job would earn you enough in that time. I said no, Becca, and that's my final word on the subject. You had a good time today. Enjoy that, then put it behind you. It's not as though you were really serious about it before today anyway. You were only going into it because of a dare, as I remember. A laugh, you told us."

"But today's changed everything," I said, getting

up to leave. "And I worked hard on that song. You just don't understand, do you?"

Neither of them said anything.

"Thanks for the support," I said and stomped off.

Upstairs I rang Cat. She sounded down as well.

"My dad says I can't go," she said. "No money and he can't leave the shop, blah, blah, won't let me go alone, blah, blah."

"Tell me about it," I said. "I've just had the 'and that's my final word on the subject' talk downstairs."

"It's not fair, is it?"

"No, it really stinks. Haven't you got *any* money, Cat?"

"Thirty quid and that's really for getting Christmas presents."

"We could do the lottery."

"I guess," said Cat. "I feel really rotten. Today was so great, and now it's like a huge anticlimax."

"I know what you mean. Like being given something really fab, then told to give it back."

"I know," said Cat. "Life sucks. I think I need chocolate."

"Yeah, me too. Still at least we break up on Thursday."

"I guess," said Cat.

"I guess," I said. "Christmas." But even the thought of that didn't cheer me up.

The next morning I grabbed my bike and headed out before the Miseries came down to ruin my life some more. I'd arranged to meet Cat and go to Lia's where at least we could commiserate in style. Lia's house is so fab and posh, it's like a fancy hotel. It has its own grounds, tennis courts, and a swimming pool. Amazingly Lia isn't spoiled or stuck-up at all about being so well off, and her mum always makes Cat and me feel really welcome. I love going there, so it was just the job for today.

On the way I couldn't help thinking what it would be like if I could go for the next round. It occurred to me that all the big stars had to start somewhere; that they were all ordinary people once, but they made it happen. Like Dad always says, because they kept trying. I bet they had obstacles to overcome, I thought as I peddled furiously up a hill.

Cat was waiting for me at the top, and we rode the rest of the way together.

"You know what, Cat?" I said after we were let in the gates, as we were cycling up the long drive to the house.

"What?"

"I think we should practice new songs for the auditions anyway."

"Why?" she asked. "What's the point?"

"We shouldn't give up. We'll pray for a miracle. You never know what might happen. My dad's always saying that when he gets a rejection for his novel—it's not over until it's over, and you must never give up. Like we were watching the World Cup once when my grandad was at our house—I can't remember who was playing—and it looked like one team had won. Then it went into extra time and in the very last ten seconds, the losing team scored a goal. Grandad was really fed up because he missed it. He'd thought his team had lost, so he'd gotten up to make a cup of tea. He'd missed the best moment in the whole match."

"Yeah, I see what you're saying," said Cat, "but—"

"No buts," I said, "and that's my final word on the subject."

"Oo, er, get *her*," said Cat. But I'd got her smiling again.

Lia was waiting for us at the top of the drive and waved when she saw us.

"I've had a brill idea," she said, beaming at us.

"So have I," I said as Cat and I leaned our bikes against the wall and followed Lia inside.

"Come upstairs and I'll tell you mine," she said.

We bounded up the stairs two at a time and into her gorgeous princess's bedroom—enormous with a bay window that has a seat in it so you can sit and look out over the fields to the sea down below, and a huge bed with a turquoise canopy.

"Okay, you first," she said as she flopped on the bed and Cat and I sat in the window seat.

"Well, I think Cat and I should learn a song anyway," I said, "even though Cat's dad and my stupid parents have said we can't go. Then we pray for a miracle. I don't know what, but you never know. Something might turn up, even if we have to hitchhike and sleep on the street."

Lia grinned at us. "I may have your miracle. I was thinking about it this morning after you phoned. No place to stay, you said. Then I thought, of course, my sister, Star."

Cat and I looked at each other and smiled. Star is Lia's elder sister. Star's a model in London. She has a *flat* in London.

"You could stay with her," said Lia. "I'm sure she wouldn't mind."

I leaped off my seat and gave Lia a hug. "Oh, do you think she'd let us? God, that would be so fab. I bet she lives somewhere amazing."

"She lives in Notting Hill Gate. It is pretty good there," said Lia. "I could phone her, but first I'd better tell Mum, even though I'm sure she'll agree. I told her all about your parents saying you couldn't go and she felt really sorry for you."

The roller-coaster ride suddenly changed direction and my hopes soared. "Ohmigod, Cat, maybe we can go after all."

Lia got up. "I'll go and ask Mum, then I'll be right back and we can phone Star. Okay?"

"Okay," we chorused as she left the room.

Cat and I had a look through Lia's CD collection while she was gone.

"I think I'd like to do the Britney Spears song," I said. "You know, the one she sings in the movie *Crossroads*, 'I'm Not a Girl, Not Yet a Woman.'"

"Oh, good choice," said Cat. "I think I'd like to do Atomic Kitten, 'Whole Again.' I know a few people did it yesterday, but I don't think that matters, does it?"

"Nah. I lost count of the number of people who did 'Rock DJ' or Kylie's 'Spinning Around.'"

The door opened as we were engrossed in the CDs. We looked up expectantly, but Lia shook her head.

"I'm so sorry, guys; I didn't know. Apparently Star's going to Bermuda for Christmas with some new bloke she's met and she's already said a couple of her friends can have the flat. I'm so sorry."

Down, down, down, my spirits sank. But then I had a flash of inspiration.

"Mac!" I said.

"Mac what?" asked Cat.

"*Mac*. Why didn't I think of it before? His dad lives in London, doesn't he?"

"Course! Let's ring him," said Cat. Then her face dropped. "Oh, but there's Jade. Jade's bound to be staying there, isn't she? She's not going to want us along."

"Yeah," I said, "But Mac's my *boyfriend*. Let's phone and see what he says."

Lia picked up the phone, dialed, and asked for Mac.

"Not there," she said as she put the phone down.

"Oh no," said Cat. "I can stand this suspense. Where is he? Bec, haven't you got his mobile number?"

But I was already on the phone and this time I got through and explained our idea.

"I was about to ring you," he said. "Mum's driving us up on Friday—Jade for the competition and me to spend some time with Dad before Christmas. I was going to tell you so that we could meet up or I could come to the audition with you. Let me ask Dad if you can stay."

"What about Jade?" I asked.

"Oh, stuff her," said Mac. "I'm sick of her at the

moment. She's obsessed with this competition and in a really bad mood all the time. I don't care what she thinks. It's if Dad says yes or no that counts."

He hung up then called back a few minutes later. "The man from Del Monte says yes," he said. "Pack your bags."

"Mac, you are *top*," I said. "Now all I've got to do is persuade the Miseries."

9 Practice Makes Perfect

"LET ME go and have a quick word with your mother," said Dad, after I'd explained the plan, the minute I got home. "You wait here."

We were sitting in his study and I could see he was weakening. "Make sure you tell her *exactly*, Dad," I said. "Mac's mum said that Cat and I could have a lift up with them, so *no* travel expenses, and we could stay at Mac's, so *no* accommodation to pay for. All I need is a bit of pocket money for the tube and, as for food, I'll starve. It's only two days. I can do it. And Cat's dad has already said that she could go as long as I was going as well, and I can't let her down, not now. Okay? Make *sure* you say that Cat's dad has said yes."

"Don't worry," said Dad, getting up from his chair. "I think I've got it all."

As I waited for Dad to come back from talking to

Mum, I had a mooch round the study. Everything I saw echoed the way I was feeling. Dad had reminders on sticky notes on his walls to inspire him. One was by a bloke called Hannibal: "We will either find a way, or make one," it said. That's right, Hannibal my man, I thought. My sentiments exactly. Another said, "The darkest hour is just before dawn." Too true. "No failure except in not trying," said another. I was beginning to feel more and more fired up as I read them.

Dad came back a few minutes later and smiled when he saw me reading the notes.

"There's some really good quotes here, Dad," I said.

"I know. Some days I need all the inspiration I can get." He walked over to his desk. "This is one of my favorites. It's by Robert Browning: 'A man's reach must exceed his grasp. Else what's a heaven for?'"

"Exactly. You got to have a dream. So? What did Mum say?"

Dad sat at his desk. "She'll be here in a moment. I'll let her tell you."

I tried to read his face for signs of the verdict, but he wasn't giving anything away. Oh please, *please* let her say yes, I prayed as Dad rummaged in his drawer and pulled out a sheet of paper.

"Look at these," he said. "It's a list of novels that were rejected by publishers. *Day of the Jackal, Tess of the D'Urbervilles, Catch 22, Animal Farm, Lord of the Flies, Wind in the Willows* . . ."

"*Wind in the Willows*?" I asked. "But we did that at junior school, and Mac is doing *Lord of the Flies* in English."

"Exactly," said Dad. "I keep this list to remind myself that even writers who have become household names had their fair share of rejections. But they persevered and got accepted in the end. Even *Harry Potter* was rejected by publishers at first."

"I think you're amazing, Dad," I said. "You've had so many rejections and you still keep at it."

"Well, believe me—there are days when I feel like packing it all in, but, well, what I wanted to say, Becca, is that you have to believe in yourself. There's a lot of competition out there, there can be a lot of obstacles to overcome on the way."

Oh dear, I thought. Is he trying to tell me that Mum's going to be an obstacle?

At that moment, the door opened and Mum came in to join us. I looked up at her hopefully. "So? Can I go?"

"If it really means so much to you, Becca," she said, "yes, you can go. But you mustn't be disappointed if nothing comes of it. I'd hate you to get all your hopes up then be let down."

I ran over to her gave her a huge hug. "Oh *top*, Mum. Thanks, thanks so much."

She smiled, then got out her purse. "We've been having a chat, your dad and I, and we've got something to put to you. It's your choice, but, well, it's Christmas soon and of course we've put a bit aside to get your presents. If you like, you can have the cash to take with you up to London. But it will mean no presents on the day."

"Oh *fantastic*. No, Mum, Dad, this is the *best* Christmas present in the world. This is what I want more than anything. And it means I won't have to starve."

Mum laughed. "We'd never let you starve, Becca. Don't be daft."

* * *

The rest of the week was brilliant. It felt as if my whole life had gone up a gear. I felt really alive. On Tuesday, Cat and I both got letters confirming our places in the next round and asking us to bring casual clothes and be prepared to stay in London if we were picked for the third round on Sunday. At school everyone was talking about the competition and when news got out that three of us had got through, we were treated like celebrities. People whispered when we walked past and one girl from Year Seven even asked for my autograph. Of course Jade was a bit sniffy with us and kept to herself. Shame, because if she'd only been a bit friendlier, Cat and I would have been as supportive of her as we were of each other. Part of it all being so fantastic was sharing it with Cat.

Cat and I practiced at every available moment. I'd never worked so hard at anything in my life— sometimes at her house, sometimes at mine, sometimes at Lia's. And Mac and Squidge came over to watch and lend their support.

"So what happens on Saturday?" asked Squidge as he filmed us rehearsing in Lia's bedroom.

"Don't know exactly," I said. "We've just been asked to come prepared with another song."

"But are they going to get the numbers down again?" he asked. "How many get through this time?"

"I think it's down to fifty next," said Cat. "Twenty-five boys and twenty-five girls. Oh, I wish you could come as well, Squidge."

Squidge shrugged and pointed at Mac. "Ah well, I have my man here to report back, and besides, that Tanya told me I had to stop filming when the real TV crews arrived last week so I couldn't have done much anyway."

"I wish I was coming as well," said Lia, "but Mum wants me here to help her get ready for Christmas. Maybe next time."

"Next time?" I asked.

"Yeah, dummy," she said. "You don't think it's all going to stop this weekend, do you? What about the next round?"

I hadn't thought about that. I'd been so focused on this weekend, I hadn't thought about what would come after that. I'd better be careful with my

Christmas money, I thought. I may need it to stretch to two weekends.

"Ohmigod. What if one of us actually won? What if we do get through into the final rounds?" I asked Cat.

"I know," she said. "It's so exciting, isn't it? Today Torpoint, tomorrow . . ."

"The world," said Squidge, grinning.

"Let's look up what your horoscope says on the Net," said Lia. "There's a brilliant site my sister told me about. Maybe it will tell us if you're going to win or not."

"Brill," said Cat. "Switch your computer on."

A few minutes later Lia had printed off our horoscopes. Aries for Cat and Pisces for me. Cat and I quickly read the sheets of paper Lia handed us.

"Ohmigod," said Cat, "December twenty-first . . . does it say anything on yours, Becca? Mine says there's a new moon on that day and that can signify the start of a new chapter. Then it says that Aries is the sign of individuality and I should be ready to shine. I'll be getting attention from some 'higher-ups.' That probably means the judges, don't you think? It doesn't say if they're going to like me or not, though. What does yours say, Bec?"

"Same. The twenty-first is a star-studded day and time of new beginning. Oh, and Venus is conjunct with the moon, meaning romance is in the air for those who are single. A meeting with new friends . . ."

"Hmm," said Mac, "don't like the sound of that. Maybe it's a good job I'm coming along to keep an eye on you."

I went over to Lia's window seat where he was sitting and put my arm around him. "Not worried about me running off with Robbie Williams, are you now?"

Mac took my hand. "Nah, course not. Now if that Enrique Iglesias was going to be there, maybe . . ."

I laughed and went back to my horoscope. It did sound promising, and I had to admit to myself that there had been some very cute boys at the last audition. It would be nice to at least get talking to some of them, and I hoped Mac wasn't going to hold me back from getting to know them by being possessive or jealous or anything. No harm in making a few new friends, I told myself.

"Well, bring a few of those boys home for me," said Lia. "I could do with a bit of romance."

"No prob," I said. I noticed that Cat wasn't saying anything. I was sure she wanted to meet new people as well, as things with Ollie weren't serious, and besides, he'd gone skiing with a bunch of mates for the Christmas holidays. But I guessed that she was being sensitive to Squidge as they'd only broken up recently. Even though they were both cool about it, she probably didn't want to hurt his feelings by being too eager about other boys.

After we'd run through our numbers a couple of times, Lia's dad popped his head around the door.

"Hey," he said, "sounds good. Lia's been telling me all about the competition. Want to show me what you're going to do?"

At first I didn't want to. I mean, he's not just any dad—he's Zac Axford, rock singer extraordinaire. Then I thought, No, if anyone can give us a few tips, it's him. So I nodded. "If you can give us advice, that would be great."

I went first and Cat and Lia clapped afterward.

"Good," said Zac. "Yeah, you have a good voice, Becca. Okay, a few tips: posture—you look terrified. Stand up straight, but try and relax. You were standing too rigidly there. Loosen up—don't hold your arms so tight to your sides, and bend your knees a little."

"I think I look rigid because I'm trying to stop my knees from shaking," I said. "It was awful in the first round."

"Ah, classic case of jelly knees," Zac said, smiling. "We all get it when we start out. Okay, I want you to sing the song again, but this time, I *want* you to shake. Shake on purpose. Sing the song and tremble, shake your arms . . ."

I started singing and did as he told me.

"Good," he said, "let those legs wobble and tremble, give in to it. Come on, really get into it, shake, shake, *shake* . . ."

I continued singing and shaking, and in the end, I couldn't help laughing as well.

"Okay, good," he said. "Now do it again. This time without the exaggerated shaking."

I did the song again and it did feel better—more

relaxed, and my knees seemed to behave themselves this time.

"Good," he said when I'd finished. "See, what you resist, persists. Don't resist it. Before you go in on Saturday, have a good shake and tremble. Let rip, wibble-wobble like mad. Shake it all out of your arms, your hands, your legs. That way, you'll get it out of your system."

Cat sang next and he had some good advice for her as well. "Okay, Cat, you sing well too," he said. "But try and put a bit more emotion into the words. Really think about what you're singing. Feel it."

By the time he'd finished with us, we both felt way better. Loads more confident.

"This time, I feel ready," I said to Cat as we cycled home together. "I can't wait."

Moaning Minnie

10

TALK ABOUT sulky! Jade insisted on going in the front on the way up to London. Mrs. Macey wanted Mac to go in the passenger seat, because he was the tallest and needed the leg room, but he said he didn't care. So Mac, Cat, and I had to squash into the back seat. Then Jade hardly said a word the whole way, except to complain.

"Could we open a window? It's too hot."

"Could we close the window? It's too cold."

"I'm hungry."

"I'm thirsty."

"I need a wee."

We didn't mind too much, though, as we had a really good laugh in the back, singing daft songs at the top of our voices. I felt great. Term was over and we were off to the big city.

"Do you mind?" said Jade at one point when we

were singing our own version of "Reach for the Sky" in Scottish accents. "Some of us are taking this competition seriously. I can't think with you lot caterwauling in the back."

Mac made a face at the back of her head and began to sing his version of "Hang the DJ" in an Indian accent.

"Mum, *Mum*, tell them, will you?" Jade whined to her mother.

"Keep it down," said Mrs. Macey, but I could see in the car mirror that she was smiling.

We tried to be quiet for a bit after that, then Cat got a fit of giggles which started me off, then Mac.

"*Mac*," moaned Jade.

"Oh shut it, prissy-pants," said Mac.

"Nappy-bucket," said Jade.

"Marsupial," said Mac. "Moaning Minnie."

"Mac, cut it out," said Mrs. Macey.

"But, *Mum*, she started it," Mac objected.

"And you're going to finish it," said Mrs. Macey. "Both of you, act your ages."

Mac pretended to dribble in the back and that set Cat and I off laughing again and Jade looked even crosser and folded her arms and legs tightly. She looked really miserable. Oops, I thought, she *really* wishes we weren't here. I used to think it would be nice to have brothers and sisters; it can be lonely being an only child sometimes. Not after today, though, after listening to Mac and Jade wind each other up like crazy. I thanked my lucky stars I was an only child.

All Jade's moaning was soon forgotten when we reached the big city. I had come up on a school trip to London from Bristol when I was about seven, but I didn't remember much. Now it looked awesome, as different to Cornwall as you could get. Like another country, I thought as I took in the traffic, the buses, the crowds hurrying home from work, the shops . . . and the *shops*. Wow. I was tempted to go and cruise them for something special to wear for the auditions, but then I reminded myself that I might get through even further in the competition so I'd better hang on to what money I had.

After a while, the heavy traffic petered out and we reached some lovely tree-lined streets with big old houses.

"This is Hampstead," said Mac. "We're almost there. Dad moved last month to a flat near the Highgate tube station, so it will be easy to travel in the morning if he can't drop us."

When we reached Mr. Macey's flat, Mrs. Macey didn't get out of the car. Mac's mum and dad had only been divorced for a year or so and it was still a bit weird between them. Mac got out and fetched the bags from the boot and Cat and I helped him carry them in. Mr. Macey came out as we unloaded and said something to Mrs. Macey while she sat stony-faced in the car. I couldn't hear what he said, but I could tell by his body language that he wasn't comfortable. Mac glanced over at them a few times. I knew he wished that they'd never got divorced because it meant he'd had to leave London and all his mates.

"You okay?" I asked as I hauled a bag on to the front steps.

He shrugged. "Yeah. Same old, same old." Then he carried the bags inside. "I'll take our stuff into our room in a mo."

I'd told Mum and Dad that Cat and I were

going to sleep on the floor in Jade's room. I don't think they'd have agreed to let me sleep in Mac's room. But he'd insisted he'd behave so we'd arranged that Cat was going to sleep on Jade's floor in her sleeping bag and Mac was going to sleep on his floor and let me have his bed.

However, as soon as we got inside, Cat came over to me and pleaded. "Don't make me sleep with her, please. Can't I come in with you and Mac?"

"Sure," I said. I wouldn't have wanted to share with Jade either. "She probably snores anyway."

"I heard that," said Jade, coming in the front door. "And I do *not* snore. And I'm very happy to have my room to myself. It wasn't *my* idea to bring you two along. Mac, Mum wants to say good-bye."

Mac went out and returned a few minutes later. His dad seemed nice and more relaxed after Mrs. Macey had driven off. He looked a lot like Mac: same dimple on his chin, blue eyes, and a friendly face. "So, you lot, what would you like to do tonight?"

"Pizza," said Mac.

"I have to rehearse," said Jade, flouncing off upstairs. "And I don't want to be disturbed."

"No problem there," said Mac.

"Pizza it is, then," said Mr. Macey. "You know I can't cook. So we'll eat, then how about I get a video?"

"Great," said Cat and I. We'd already decided we'd go over the songs once that night, then we'd relax so we were fresh for the morning.

Everything was going really well until bedtime. Cat and I went up and got changed, and Mac stayed downstairs to catch up with his dad. When he came up half an hour later, he didn't look happy.

"What's up?" I asked.

"Nothing," he said. But he looked really down. What on Earth could have happened in half an hour? I wondered.

"Come on, Mac," said Cat. "Spill. We're your mates, you can tell us."

Mac sat on the end of the bed. "Oh, it's probably nothing. Just, well, Dad's gone and got himself a stupid girlfriend. He wants Jade and me to go out with him tomorrow night and meet her. I don't want to go."

"Why not?" I asked. "She might be really nice."

"Nah," said Mac. "She's causing problems already. Like I've come up here to see my dad and already he's saying I have to make my own arrangements for Sunday night. Apparently she's an actress and he's going to some play and after-production party with her. I mean, what's the point of coming up to see him if he's not going to be here? Then it'll be Monday and Mum will be back to pick us up."

"Well, we're here," I said, snuggling up to him.

"Yeah, but you won't always be. And I can just see it. I know exactly what's going to happen. He'll start canceling my visits. I'll be in the way. He'll probably marry her and have more babies and they'll take my room and then they won't want me around anymore, ever."

"You sound like Puddleglum the marsh-wiggle in the Narnia books," I said. "Only seeing the worst. Come on, Mac, it might not be so bad. You might like her."

"Yeah," said Cat. "Like when Dad first started going out with Jen, I was all like, Ohmigod, I don't know if I like this, but it turned out to be the best thing ever. She's great and it's good to see Dad happy again. Parents have to get on with their lives as well."

"Yeah but your mum died," said Mac. "My mum and dad got divorced so it's different. And what about Mum? Now she'll never have him back."

"Does she want him back?" I asked.

"Well, not at the moment," said Mac. "But I thought it was only a matter of time. They used to get on really well. Now this has ruined everything."

Sometimes advice is not what's required, I thought as I put my arms round him. Sometimes all you need is a hug and something to distract you. Poor Mac. It's not like him to be sulky and negative, but then I don't think I'd like it if my mum and dad split up and had new partners either. God, I hope it doesn't happen. Mustn't think those thoughts, I told myself. I have to be positive for the morning.

"Come on," I said, climbing into bed as Mac struggled to get comfortable in his sleeping bag on the floor. "Let's all sleep on it. Big day tomorrow. Now, who's going to tell the first ghost story?"

Round Two

11

"WHAT I said about the judges being nice the first time . . . ," I said to Cat when we caught up at the lunch break the next day. "I take it back."

"Tell me about it," she said gloomily.

Mr. Macey had dropped us off at the hall behind Tottenham Court Road at nine o'clock. It was now twelve and the last three hours were possibly the most excruciating of my whole life.

After we'd arrived and registered, we were separated from the boys and split into groups of five. Then we were asked to go in, one group at a time, to see the judges. Sadly, Cat wasn't in my group; happily, Jade wasn't either. When we got in the hall, we all had to troop up onto the stage and stand there with the spotlight on us. It was awful— the judges didn't say anything, just looked us up and down like we were contestants at a pet show, then they all wrote stuff on pads of paper in front of them. I felt like doing something really stupid at one point, like flashing my chest at them, then I saw that a camera crew had set up at the back of the hall and decided that my parents wouldn't be too happy if they saw me doing something daft like that on telly.

When the judges had all had a good stare at us, they dimmed the lights, and one by one we were called to sing our song, in front of each other as well as in front of the camera and judges. I was third up and was feeling intimidated, as the two girls before me were good, and I mean *really* good. The one after me was okay and the fifth one blew it all together. Worst of all, though, was that at the end of our performances the judges made no comment. I'd prepared myself for the usual insults, but total silence was much worse. Nothing. Not a "good," a "bad," or a "you're ugly." They just told each group, "We'll let you know this afternoon when we've seen everyone."

After that, everyone had to go and have lunch in a room on the first floor. It felt like we were at a funeral, not a pop competition. No one was popping here, not anymore. We'd done our bubbly bit, now everyone looked anxious and deflated. Not surprising, really, considering what we'd been though.

Cat and I took a sandwich and an apple juice from the table and went to sit on a bench in a corner to talk over the events of the morning.

"Well, at least we get free bread and butter this time." Cat smiled weakly.

"Consolation prize," I said. "Not a Grammy, but a cheese-and-tomato sarnie. Yeah, at least we'll have something to show for our efforts. So how did you get on?"

"Crap, crap, crapola," said Cat, shaking her head. "It really threw me when we had to get up in groups of five."

"I know," I said. "It felt weird to be compared to one another like that."

"I guess they were looking to see if anyone stood out with star quality. I just wish I'd been in a group with smaller girls. I felt really conspicuous. All the girls in my group were tall with legs up to their armpits."

"Kylie's tiny and Madonna's not much taller," I said. "They won't hold your height against you. Better to be tiny than enormous like me!" I said.

"Becca!" said Cat. "You're not enormous. You may not be a size eight, but you're not enormous. You're normal."

"Can I join you?" said a voice to our left.

I looked up to see a boy I'd noticed on the way in. He was dark, with spiky hair and he was very, very good-looking.

"Sure," I said.

"Thanks," he said, taking a seat next to Cat. "I don't know anyone in this round and boy, I feel like I need to talk to someone."

"Know what you mean," said Cat. "How were the boys' groups?"

"Tense. It's like the stakes have gone way up, you know. If you don't cut it, then *kaput*. I'm Elliott, by the way."

"Cat and Becca," said Cat.

"How was your session?" he asked.

"About as much fun as having your arm ripped off," I said.

"And being hit with the soggy end," said Cat.

I started laughing then. "So much for my fantasy about being on *Top of the Pops*. It'll more likely be *Top of the Flops*."

"I dunno," said Elliott. "Who knows what they're looking for? Weren't they happy with your song?"

"Hard to say. It helped having the lights turned down," I said. "Then I couldn't see the three monkeys in front of me. You know, see no evil, hear no evil, speak no evil. They didn't say a word. I tried to imagine I was in my mate's room back home and that helped a bit."

"So what happens now?" said Cat. "They've seen half of us so I guess it's going to take as long again to see the next lot."

Elliott nodded. "Yeah. We wait. And we wait. And we wait. That's why I thought I'd come and introduce myself. Didn't want to sit here on my own, imagining the worst. So, anyone want another stale sandwich?"

We both shook our heads, and he got up and went back to the food table. Cat nudged me. "Cute, huh?"

"*Très* cute," I said. I'd felt a bit rotten this morning when they wouldn't allow Mac to come in with us. He'd been sent away at the door with all the other friends and relatives and told to come back at four o'clock. So instead he'd gone off to catch up with some of his old mates. Now I was almost glad he wasn't there. I'd have a chance to get to know the gorgeous Elliott. Fickle is thy name, Becca, I thought to myself. But I'm only going to talk to him. . . .

There's a saying that goes something like, "Time is too short for those who rush, too long for those who wait." I looked at the clock again. I could have sworn it hadn't moved since the last time I glanced up. It was like the room was standing still and the moment had become eternal. We'd learned all that we could about Elliott. Fifteen years old, Aquarius, from Manchester, three sisters, both parents teachers, staying with his aunt in Crouch End. Hobbies: tennis, surfing the Net, movies, wants to be—what else?—a pop star, plays the guitar, fave film: *Road Trip*.

He got the same rundown about us. We talked endlessly about the other competitions and who we'd wanted to win on *Pop Idol*. By midafternoon, I felt I'd known Elliott all my life.

Elliott seemed to know all about the judges. "Martin Riley," he said. "He's the older one. He's a DJ and he's been involved in the music business for years. Rumor has it, he puts up a lot of money to sponsor new bands. The one with glasses is Paul Parker—he's a producer. He's got some brill bands on his list. And the woman is Sarah Hardman—she manages the bands on Paul Parker's list."

"So, which of them do you think is going to be the bad guy?" I asked.

"Martin," said Elliott. "He's already laid into a few of the boys for wasting their time."

"Thought so," I said. "He wasn't going to let me through the first round, but the other two voted him out. Wonder what he wrote about me this morning."

As the clock hit half past three, Cat sighed. "No sign of Jade. She must be in with the afternoon groups. So what shall we do? How about we play I Spy?"

"I spy with my little eye, fifty worried-looking teenagers," I said. "It's weird, though, with all this waiting, I feel like I've gone from anxiety to excitement to anxiety, and now I feel, oh, so what?"

At that moment, Tanya came in and clapped her hands for silence. "All the girls, please go into the main hall," she said.

My "oh, so what?" feeling suddenly evaporated and my tummy tightened into a knot. It was back to "oh God," "oh argggh," "oh yeah," "oh *no*." I think I may be cracking up, I thought as I followed the others in and wondered if they were all feeling as barking mad as I was.

All fifty girls went up on stage and I stood in a line at the back with Cat.

"Okay, it's cut-down time," said Paul, getting up. "Some of you are going to go forward to the next round. Some of you, we won't be asking back. First, I'd like to say we've seen some great talent here today and you should all be very proud of yourselves. . . ."

"Blah, blah," Cat whispered. "Get *on* with it."

"So I'm going to call some names," Paul continued.

"When I've finished, I want those girls to step forward and the rest of you to stay where you are."

"Ohmigod," I said. "Here we go—prolong the agony."

The roll call began and girls began to step forward. It was deathly quiet as no one knew which group would be carrying on and which were finished—the girls being called forward or those staying put.

"Cat Kennedy," called Paul.

Cat squeezed my arm. "Nice knowing yous, *amigo*," she said as she left to take her place at the front.

The roll call continued, and I realized they were doing it alphabetically. They got to the *M*s, but didn't call Jade Macey. She'd get through, surely. And the girl that hit the bum notes in my group was one of the ones called forward. Ohmigod, did that mean I was through again? I felt like my brain was going to fuse. Maybe? . . . Maybe not? . . . Maybe? It would be fantastic. But then that would mean that Cat didn't get through. Not so fantastic. The suspense was unbearable. When Paul had reached the final name, Martin got up.

"As Paul said," he started, "we've seen some amazing talent here today. It's been really hard coming to a decision. But after seeing you all today, it's become clear that some of you definitely are *not* our Pop Princess, some of you gave borderline performances, and some of you were terrific. But a Pop Princess can never be borderline. You could never describe Madonna, Anastacia, or Kylie Minogue as borderline. They've got the X-factor and you know it. So the group at the back . . ." He paused and looked toward the back of the stage. My heart sank. So I hadn't got through. Then Martin smiled and went on, ". . . well done. We're going to ask you to come back tomorrow, nine a.m. sharp. The group at the front, I'm afraid we won't be asking you back, but thanks for coming and well done everybody."

There was a huge sigh of relief from the back, then cheers as girls started jumping up and down and hugging each other. I went straight over to Cat and gave her a huge hug.

"God. Sorry, Cat," I said.

She shrugged. "I kind of knew I wouldn't get through. I knew I was crapola today. You know it in your bones when it's not your best. But, *hey*, well done, you."

"Yeah, I guess," I said. But somehow it didn't feel like last time when we'd gotten through together.

12 Journey Into Hell

"WHERE'S JADE?" I asked early the next morning when I walked into the kitchen.

"In her room," said Mac. "She's about to leave, so I said I'd take you if you want to grab a bit of toast or something."

"Yeah, best to eat something as you've got a long day ahead," said Cat. "I'll come with you as well. Mac and I are going to go down to Spitalfields Market."

"God, I wish I could come with you," I said. "I'd love to go there."

"And I'd love to be coming with you," said Cat, putting a piece of bread in the toaster. "Now do you want to run through the song they gave you one more time?"

"Nah, I've been thinking about it all night. I haven't slept a wink, hardly. I kept dreaming I was doing exams, but hadn't done any studying. Then I dreamed I was standing on stage naked. Honestly, this was supposed to be fun, but it's turning out to be even worse than school."

The twenty-five girls chosen to go back the next day had all been asked to stay behind for five minutes after the judges' verdict, then we'd been given song sheets to learn overnight and have ready for the morning. I'd been given "Wind Beneath My Wings," by Bette Midler, and I felt overwhelmingly nervous.

"Well, what did you expect?" said Jade, coming in behind us. "I don't even know why you bothered coming up this time, Becca. Mac told me you only did it because Squidge dared you. Some other girl who was serious about it could have had your place instead of you wasting the judges' time."

"Oh, leave off, Jade," said Cat. "Loads of people entered, for all sorts of reasons. And Becca wouldn't have got this far if she wasn't good."

"Well, that's a matter of opinion," she said. "Anyway, I'm off. See you there if you can be bothered to turn up."

"See you," I said, then thought, And thanks so much for all the support and encouragement. I'd been ready to be really sympathetic today, as I felt sorry for her, having to go out for dinner with her dad the night before. Not because he was going to be introducing his new girlfriend, but because I knew she had a song to learn as well. I'd been lucky—I had Cat to help me go over mine and an empty flat to practice in while Mr. Macey, Jade, and Mac were out. Jade went into her room to rehearse the minute she got back and I could still hear her every time I woke up from my bad dreams, so she can't have got much sleep either. Maybe that was why she was double ratty.

"Take no notice of her," said Cat after Jade had left. "She's probably feeling threatened because you *are* good and she knows it."

"Thanks," I said. "At least you believe in me. I'd far prefer traveling with you two to getting slagged off by her for the whole journey."

After a quick bite of toast and some tea, we set off for the tube station. I looked at my watch. We had an hour, plenty of time to get to Tottenham Court Road, as the journey only took about half an hour.

"So, new girlfriend?" I asked. "Any more thoughts this morning?"

"I'll see how it goes," said Mac. Last night he'd seemed reticent to say much when he got back, and I didn't want to push him. Mac wasn't someone you could make talk if he didn't want to. He opened up when and if he was ready.

"Well, I hope you were nice to her," said Cat. "I bet it was hard for her too, meeting your dad's kids."

"I was polite," said Mac.

"She probably just wants to get on with you," I said. "I think you should give her a break."

"Hmphh," said Mac.

When we got to Highgate tube station, the next train wasn't for fifteen minutes.

"Bugger," said Mac. "I should have remembered. Trains are always less frequent on a Sunday. That's probably why Jade went early; she must have remembered and didn't want to take any chances. Shouldn't be a problem, though. We've still got time."

I tried to make myself relax and mentally ran through the words of the song as we waited. Then Cat made me do Zac's "shake it out" routine, which got a few funny looks from some of the people waiting at the station. Thankfully, the train arrived when it was supposed to and we all got on.

"We'll make it," said Mac, glancing at his watch, "so you can chill out now."

Phew, I thought, at last we're on our way. I'll get there just in time.

Then the train stopped at Camden.

"Oh God, what's happening now?" I asked after we'd been sitting there for a few minutes.

"This train is no longer in service," said an announcement. "All change please. If you are traveling farther south, go to the Charing Cross branch and continue your journey from there."

"What does that mean?" I asked Mac as we got off the train.

"It means we run like hell through the tunnel," said Mac setting off at a pace. "The other line."

He began to run up some steps, so we followed him, then through a tunnel and down some more steps.

"Next train in eight minutes," I said. I checked my watch. "Oh God, it's a quarter to nine. I'm going to be late."

"We might just make it," said Mac, but even he was beginning to look worried. "The Northern Line. Londoners call it the misery line—now you know why."

I arrived at the hall at twelve minutes past nine.

"We'll meet you outside later," Cat called after me as I hurried inside.

The foyer was deserted, so I ran toward the hall. As I pushed the door open, everyone turned to look, including Martin Riley. And he didn't look pleased.

The boys and girls were in separate halls again and the judges split their time between the two.

By midafternoon, I'd had enough. Martin definitely had it in for me. After a dressing down for being late, in front of *everyone*, he'd taken every opportunity to slag me off.

10:00 a.m.: "You sound like you're singing along with the radio."

11:10 a.m.: "It's all on one level, Becca. Start quietly, build. Put some emotion into it. You sound like you're singing, 'I had eggs for breakfast.' It's that boring."

12:00 p.m.: "Breathe, Becca, breathe."

1:30 p.m.: "Nah, not good enough, start again."

2:15 p.m.: "You're holding yourself too tight. Relax, let it come from your abdomen, not your throat."

3:00 p.m.: "Come *on*, Becca, impress me."

I got worse and worse as the day progressed and by the end I had the confidence of a timid amoeba. On the other hand, the real stars were beginning to stand out. Jade performed brilliantly, as did an Indian girl called Sushila, and a small blond girl called Fizz.

"They're going to let another twenty go today," whispered a blond girl as we went to stand around a piano to sing with accompaniment for the fifth time that day. "Ten boys and ten girls."

"Good," I whispered back. "I hope I'm one of the ones they let go."

She gave me a strange look, but I meant it. I could have been out having a good time with Cat and Mac all day, but instead I was locked in a strange hall with a load of people I didn't know, being put through physical and mental torture. We'd had to sing solo, sing in groups, sing solo again with the piano . . . I was tired and hoarse and my feet hurt like hell from a dance session with a choreographer in which we had to prance about to "It's Raining Men." It wasn't fun anymore. I felt so alone. Although Elliott had got through, I didn't have a chance to talk to him, as the boys were shunted off into another hall to perform. I looked for him at the lunch break, but he was busy with a group of lads, practicing for the afternoon.

At the afternoon break, I took an apple juice from the table, then I looked for Jade, in the hope that she'd have chilled out since the morning. She was at the back of the room with Fizz and looked like she was having a great time practicing the dance steps we'd been taught in the morning. Of course she had them down to perfection. I went and collapsed in the corner of the room to call Cat on my mobile.

"Hey, Pop Princess," said Cat, when she answered her phone. "How's it going?"

"Get me *out* of here," I said.

Cat laughed.

"No, seriously, it's awful here today. Torture. Where are you?"

"We're in Camden Lock," said Cat. "It's fantastic, amazing. We did Spitalfields this morning, and caught the tube back up here. You'd love it. It's buzzing."

"I'll be there in half an hour. Where should I meet you?"

"Why? Has it finished already?"

"No. But *I* have Cat, I've had it."

"You've been voted out?"

"No."

"So why do you want to leave?"

"I told you, it's torture. I can't do it, Cat, and that Martin Riley's got it in for me."

"Just a mo, Mac wants to know what's happening."

The phone went quiet for a moment, and I could just about hear Cat saying something to Mac. He came on the phone a moment later.

"You must be out of your mind, Becca," he said. "You've got this far—you *can't* give up now."

I felt like crying. "But you don't understand. . . ."

Cat came back on the phone. "Why do you want to leave, Becca? You were so into it all before."

"I know, but there's loads of people here who

are better than I am. And I'm having a horrible time. I know I won't win, so why not quit while I'm still ahead."

I could hear Cat sigh heavily at the other end of the phone. "Typical," she said. "This is so totally typical of you, Becca."

"What do you mean?"

"Giving up the minute things get hard. Well, I think it's rotten of you. You've got a real problem— you know that, don't you? You can't see how good you are. It's only your fear that's holding you back. Fear of failure, fear of rejection. You'll never get anywhere if you give into it all the time."

I was taken aback. I'd never heard Cat cross at me before. "Well, it's not just that," I said. "I don't know anyone here . . ."

"You know the gorgeous Elliott; go and talk to him."

"Who's Elliott?" I heard Mac ask in the background.

"He's been busy all day," I said. "And it's like, me and you, we were in this together and it was all a laugh, but now you're out and . . ."

"Don't use me as an excuse, Becca."

"I'm not, Cat, honest. It's not an excuse. And you don't know what it's been like today. Why put myself through more misery when I know I don't stand a chance?"

"You *do* stand a chance, Becca. You're good and you just might win if you stop this whining."

I felt tears prick the back of my eyes. "You just don't understand, Cat," I said, then I hung up. I felt really miserable. I thought at least my *friends* would understand.

I reached into my rucksack to find a tissue and when I looked up, Elliott was coming over to join me. I took a big sniff and smiled so he wouldn't see that I'd been near to tears. He flopped down beside me. "Rough day, huh?"

I nodded.

"I think loads of people are ready to drop out," he said.

"Really?"

"Yeah. When the going gets tough . . . et cetera."

"Yeah, the not-so-tough get going," I said. "Me included."

"Feeling down?"

I nodded. "This place is freezing and I'm so *tired*."

"I don't think anyone slept. That's why everyone's feeling so fragile, and it doesn't help that the judges are coming down really heavy on everyone today."

"Tell me about it. That Martin Riley's been horrible to me."

"Not just you, Becca. Everyone. See, I reckon what they're doing today is testing our staying power. I mean, this is for real. Whoever wins is going to have to be serious about it, not flaky. So I reckon that's why they're pushing everyone today, to see who will crack and who can go the distance."

Suddenly I remembered what Dad had said. "Success is fifty percent talent, fifty percent perseverance."

"Right," said Elliott. "Anyway, got to go practice. Catch you later."

I took a look around the hall. It was true. Everyone did look shattered, not just me. And it had helped talking to Elliott. I felt myself starting to get fired up again. So, they were testing everybody, were they? I'd show them who was flaky and who was not. I got up to go and splash my face with cold water.

In the loos, I found Sushila in tears.

"Hey," I said, and went over to put my arm around her.

"Sorry," she sniffed. "Just . . ."

"I know," I said. "Tough today. But don't let it put you off. I was just talking to a mate and we reckon that today's all about seeing who's going to crack. Don't let them get to you. You were great up there this morning. You really stood out. All you have to do is get through another hour and it'll get better."

"You reckon? I'm just about ready to walk," she said.

"I was too. But let's show them we're made of stronger stuff, eh? You're good—you can't give up now."

She gave me a weak smile. "Thanks. And I thought you were good as well—loads better than some of the others. I'm Sushila, by the way."

"Becca," I said, and remembered another of Dad's inspirational lines. "My quote for the day is

'Fortune favors the brave.' So come on, let's get out there and strut our stuff."

The rest of the afternoon flew by. When the judges said something critical, I didn't take it personally—it spurred me on. I listened, but instead of thinking, Oh no, they think I'm crapola, I thought, Okay, how can I use that to improve my performance? Ha, I *am* professional, I thought, not a dreamer, or a flaky flake. I *can* do it.

At the end of a group session around the piano, Sarah Hardman pulled me to one side.

"Well done, Becca," she said. "I've been watching you, and you've done really well today. I know Martin's given you a bit of a rough time, but you haven't let it get to you. And don't be afraid of the criticism; it's to help, not to hinder. It's got to a lot of people today and they've gone under. Three people have dropped out already. Understandable, but I say there's no crime in falling, only in refusing to get up again. And I saw you get up a few times after Martin had his say. That's just what we're looking for. Being a Pop Princess isn't all about glamour. Whoever wins may get knocked by the press, the public . . . It can all turn from nice to nasty in an instant, and we need to know that our winner can take it."

When I heard later that I'd made it through into the last fifteen girls, I felt fantastic. Nothing is going to stop me, I thought. I'm going to go for this. I'm going to show them all. Cat, Mac, Jade, Mum, Dad, Mr. Walker . . . I may be a dreamer, but I've got what it takes to make a dream come true.

Christmas Sulks

13

MAC HAD been in a sulk for days, partly because he knew Elliott had been phoning every day to see how things were going—no matter what I told him, Mac wouldn't believe that Elliott and I were "just good friends"—and partly because he'd been in a funny mood ever since London. Meeting Sonia, his dad's new girlfriend, had given him a bit of an abandonment complex, even though no one was planning on deserting him. Certainly not me and, I'm pretty sure, not his dad.

"I'm not going to go off with Elliott," I tried to reassure him when he came over on Christmas Eve to give me my present. "For one thing, he lives in Manchester, and for another, *you're* my boyfriend. But if you keep acting so jealous for no reason, you're going to drive me away."

It was obviously the wrong thing to say because it made him sulk even more and he went off in a huff before I'd had time to open my present or give him his. Good job, really, because he gave me Anastacia's new CD, *exactly* what I'd got him. At least it gave me the chance to swap presents and labels around, so he'd get the Eminem CD that I'd bought for Squidge instead.

Mac had written "To my top Pop Princess" on the label of my present. It was a shame he was weirded out because he can be so sweet when he wants to be. I'm beginning to understand why mega-stars have difficulties with relationships. It's because their partners don't trust them when they're out meeting new glam people all the time. I hoped I wouldn't have to resort to buying a dog for company, like Geri Halliwell did in her "lonely" phase . . . although, on second thought, maybe a dog is a good idea. They're always pleased to see you and are less trouble than boys, as you don't have to explain yourself to them all the time. But I wasn't ready to give up on Mac just yet. I decided I wouldn't let him sulk for long, I'd just give him a little space, then go to his place and win him over.

Mum was in a sulk with me too on Christmas day, because I wouldn't have roast potatoes with our Christmas dinner, nor any pudding, which she said she made with extra pecans and cherries especially for me.

"You're going to waste away if you don't eat properly," she said.

No point in saying anything, I decided as I picked at my turkey. She just doesn't get it. If I want to win this competition, I have to lose half a stone at least. All the other finalists, except for one tubby girl, are stick insects. Pop icons are skinny and wear really tight jeans, often with their belly buttons showing. I knew I had to be skinny.

So far, I'd lost two pounds and I'd put all my Christmas chocolates away until the competition was over, when I could get together with Cat and Lia for a chocfest. At least Dad understands, I thought—not so much about losing weight, but about needing to be serious about the competition. No one could be more serious than he is about succeeding. He's still working away on his novel.

The rowing was still going on, though. It was awful. I could hear them sometimes when they thought I'd gone to sleep and it was always about the same thing: money, money, money. Poor Dad. It was supposed to be the season of goodwill and Mum wouldn't get off his case.

Cat came over in the evening. She was in a sulk with me too, but mainly because I'd been slightly in a sulk with her since that talk in London about never seeing anything through. It's hard staying mad at Cat, though. She was right, anyway. I made it one of my New Year's resolutions to take criticism on the chin, as long as it's constructive. And besides, Cat bought me a gorgeous black strappy top for Christmas, perfect for wearing at the next round of the competition and loads nicer than the glitter bath gels I gave her. I hadn't had much time to shop, as I'd been busy rehearsing. I'd gone to Plymouth with Mum on one of her grocery buying trips and done it all in one mad dash so I could get back to practice.

"Should I do one of the songs I've written for the next round?" I asked.

"*Nff-NO!*" said Cat through a mouthful of mince pie.

"Why not?"

"Er, um, best to stick to songs that are well-known. Um . . . like, remember Darius on *Popstars*? He wanted to do his own thing and the judges didn't appreciate it, said he was corny. He got the message to 'play the game' and he came back and did really well in *Pop Idol.* It was only later he had his number-one hit with his own song. No, Bec, you're better off singing songs they recognize."

I decided to let it go and not take offense, but I had a sneaky feeling that Cat didn't think much of my lyrics. Perhaps she's right again, I thought. Best to stick to what the judges know, as there's standing out in a good way and standing out in a naff way, and I don't want to do that.

Lia and Squidge had both been really cool since London. They came over on Boxing Day and I was really touched by their Chrissie presents.

"Wow," I said as I opened the envelopes they gave me and found two crisp ten pound notes. "Cash."

Lia smiled. "I know it's a bit boring, but we knew

that you probably need some money for your next trip to London. Don't want it to be a problem with your parents again."

"No, wow, *thanks*," I said. "No, this is top. Exactly what I need, because I've spent all the Christmas money I had left from Mum and Dad on buying all my presents for you lot. Luckily my gran and grandad sent me some dosh, but with this as well, it shouldn't be a problem at all."

"So when are you off next?" asked Squidge.

"Weekend after New Year."

"Have you decided what song you're going to do?" asked Lia.

"I thought I might do 'Endless Love' or 'Total Eclipse of the Heart.' What do you think?"

"'Endless Love,'" said Lia.

"'Total Eclipse,'" said Squidge at the same time.

I laughed. "Thanks. Or how about I combine them into 'Endless Eclipse'?"

"Sing both of them for us," said Squidge, "then we'll vote."

I stood up and sang both songs for them.

They looked genuinely impressed. "Wow," said

Squidge when I'd finished, "you're getting really good. You're loads more confident now."

"Yeah," said Lia, "*really* good."

I smiled. "Thanks. So which one?"

"'Total Eclipse,'" said Lia.

"'Endless Love,'" said Squidge.

I laughed. "Oh, that's really helpful."

In the end, we went over to Cat's house and gave her the casting vote. I think she was quite chuffed that I did value her opinion. She decided on "Endless Love." And she lent me a pair of diamond stud earrings that her mum gave to her before she died, to wear for luck. Lia lent me a pair of strappy shoes to wear. "More glam than trainers," she said. I have the best mates, I thought, they're being really brilliant. I just wished that Mac would chill out and be happy for me as well.

For the rest of the week, I practiced every spare moment I had. When the others were off somewhere hanging out or watching videos, I stayed home and rehearsed. When I wasn't rehearsing, I jogged to get fit, so that I could keep up if they made us do any more dance sessions. I drank loads of water to make sure my skin was good. And I made sure I got to bed reasonably early every night, so I looked youthful and fresh. It's a full-time business, aiming for the top.

My parents didn't know what to think. I don't think either of them had ever seen me work so hard, but I knew the next round would be the toughest. There were fifteen girls and fifteen boys left in the competition, and the judges were going to lose five of each.

"I think it's great that you're really going for this," said Dad one afternoon when I took him a cup of tea in his study. "But I'm worried that you're going to take it hard if you don't get through—you know, after having come so far."

I read him the quote he had on his wall. "'A man's reach should exceed his grasp. Else what's a heaven for?' That's your favorite, isn't it?"

That silenced him and he gave me a hug. "I'm very proud of you," he said, "and will be, whether you win or not."

Actually we'd had a few brilliant conversations since London. He understood about going for what you want and I was feeling really close to him. I grew to admire him a lot. He'd had a lot of setbacks, like I did from Martin Riley, but he kept getting up and trying again and again.

On New Year's Eve, I went over to Mac's. I was determined to get him smiling again. It was freezing outside and even looked like it might snow, but I wrapped up warmly, then cycled over and threw a stone up at his window.

"I've come to serenade you," I called up when he opened the window.

He laughed. "Like *Romeo and Juliet*?" he asked. "But isn't it supposed to be me down there and you up here on a balcony?"

"Hey," I said, "this is the twenty-first century. Things change." Then I sang "Endless Love" for him. It was hysterical, because Jade opened her window as well, but shut it as soon as she heard it was me, then the neighbor's dog came and sat on the lawn next to me and joined in, barking away with great enthusiasm.

Mac was killing himself laughing. "Enough,

enough," he said. "I'll come down and let you in."

He let me in and I followed him up the stairs to his room. "So, do you think I stand a chance?" I asked.

"Always did," he said, going into his bedroom and lying back on his bed. "But I'd lose the doggy accompaniment. I tell you something, Becca. I've been thinking about it a lot. You *do* stand a chance. I always thought you had a cracking voice, but, well, if you *do* win, you might not enjoy it as much as you think you will. Like, already you've changed. I never thought you would, but you're getting like Jade lately. This whole thing, it's become more like an obsession than a dream, for both of you. You don't want to hang out anymore, you're always rehearsing, it's all you ever talk about. The rest of us have still got lives and stuff going on, you know."

I felt hurt. "I know. And I know I haven't exactly been around. But this is important."

"And we're not?"

"The others don't seem to mind," I said. "And it's only for a few more weeks."

"Yeah, we'll see. And what if you win?"

"It'd be great."

"No, it wouldn't," he said. "It'll be more and more of the same. You'll change, your life will change. I watched *Pop Idol* too, you know, and it's obvious to anyone with half a brain who came out as the real winners."

"Yeah. Will Young and Gareth Gates," I said.

"No," said Mac. "Think about it, Becca. They were just like pawns in a chess game. They have no control. They're being molded and shaped, told what to sing, what to say and what to wear by the record companies."

"Yeah. But a *professional* makeover. I'd love it. In fact I think the stylists are coming in next time."

Mac shrugged. "If you want to be a puppet in someone else's show, then go right ahead. But the ones that make all the money and have all the say are the producers and the management team, not the artists."

"It's not like that, Mac," I said. "You don't understand."

Mac's face clouded. "And Elliott does, I suppose," he said.

"Yes, actually he does," I said, and headed for the door. I had been planning to drag him off to Squidge's to meet up with the others to see the New Year in. But come midnight, no way was I going to snog such a cynical old misery.

Complications

I THOUGHT it was all sorted. Got the song. Got the dosh. Got a place to stay . . . or so I thought until Mac put a spanner in the works.

"But I thought it was all arranged," I said when he phoned the Thursday before I was due to go up to London. "I go up with you and Jade with your mum again and . . ."

"I know. But . . . well, it's gotten complicated. Apparently Sonia has a daughter Tamara and she's going to be staying at dad's. I told you this would happen. I've read about it. Parents get divorced, one has a new family, and they become more important. . . ."

"But you don't know that. Did your dad actually say you couldn't stay?" I asked. I couldn't believe his own dad would stop him from visiting.

"Not exactly," said Mac. "That is, well, he does

want me to go, said he wants Tamara to meet me and Jade. But he can stuff it. I'm not going to go and be all pally and big brothery with someone I don't even know. I don't want to hang out with some eight-year-old kid, or her mother. Hopefully this thing with Sonia will run its course and she'll clear off so we can get back to normal."

"And what if she doesn't?" I asked. "What if they, like, really make a go of it? You'll have to get to know them sometime."

"Yeah, well, not going. Sorry. No way, José," said Mac. "But I did ask if you could stay even though I won't be there, but apparently Jade has told some other girl from the competition—Tizz or Fizz or somebody, I think her name is—that she could stay, so there isn't room."

I could feel myself starting to panic. What was I going to do? I had to get there, even if it meant sleeping on the streets.

"Maybe I could get a lift up with Jade and your mum anyway, then I'll try and find a B&B or something. Mum and Dad needn't know. If I told them I wasn't staying with you, they might stop me going, so . . . oh pants. I could still get a lift, couldn't I?"

"Er, well, that's the other thing," said Mac. "Mum's not driving Jade up. She's gone already; Mum put her on the train this morning and Dad's meeting her at the other end. God, I'm sorry, Bec. I know I was heavy the other night, but I didn't mean for any of this to happen. I didn't plan it or anything. I feel rotten for you."

He did sound genuinely bad about it so it was hard to be cross. I'd save that for Jade. I wouldn't put it past her to have invited Fizz to spite me and ruin my chances.

"Don't worry, Mac," I said. "I'll sort something out."

"But you can't stay in a B&B on your own, Becca," he said. "You said your dad's been great. Ask if he'll go with you just this once."

I sighed. "Not after this morning, I don't think."

"Why? What happened this morning?"

"I came down to breakfast and Dad was wearing a suit."

"So?" said Mac.

"A *suit*, Mac," I said. "He's gone for a job interview. Some crapola job in a college that he doesn't even want. It's just to keep my mum happy and stop her nagging him. He looked so sad. I felt awful for him. It's not what he wants. He's given up. That's another reason I have to go and do this competition—to remind him of everything he's told me over the last few weeks. Don't give up, don't give up, don't give up."

"Okay then," said Mac. "I know it will be difficult, but call Jade this evening and ask if you can kip on the floor with Fizz. She can't possibly be so hard-hearted to say no. I mean, you are all in this together. Or do you want me to ring and try again?"

"No, no," I said. "I'll think of something and if I do have to ask Jade, better that it comes from me."

At first I thought, No way I'm going crawling to Jade, but as the day went on, I realized it was my only choice. I'd have let her stay if I had a dad in London, even though we didn't get on. It was either call or not go, so I bit the bullet and dialed the number.

"Oh, but slight problem, Becca," she said after I'd

eaten humble pie. "See, Fizz will be here and there's really not room for both of you as well as Sonia's kid."

"But couldn't you just squeeze me in? Please. I'll sleep in a corner somewhere."

"Er, just a minute, Becca. Just got to do something," said Jade, then the phone went dead. Maybe she's changed her mind, I thought hopefully as I waited for her. A moment later, I heard a click and Jade came back on the line.

"I wanted to ask you something," she said. "Just between you and me. I don't really know this Fizz girl very well and she's coming here to stay and everything. You've seen her about. Do you think it will be okay? What do you think of her?"

"I don't really know," I said, wondering why she was asking me of all people and why she was even having Fizz to stay if she was having doubts about it. "I don't really know her."

"Yeah, well what do you think of her chances, you know as, Pop Princess?"

It was the first time Jade had asked for my opinion about anything to do with the competition so I took a moment to think about it. Knowing Jade, she'd want me to say something about her standing more of a chance than her new friend. Maybe if I played along, she'd let me stay.

"I think she has a really strong voice," I said. "Yeah, I think she stands a good chance, but she's not as good as you."

"But do you think she looks the part?" asked Jade.

That I could answer easily. I had noticed Fizz because of her voice, but she wasn't exactly gorgeous; in fact she was a bit weird-looking in a Marge Simpson kind of way.

"I think she needs to make more of herself image-wise," I said. "I think they're looking for a Pop Princess in every way, you know. . . ."

"What do you mean?" urged Jade.

"Well, I guess what I'm trying to say is that even though it shouldn't matter, I think it does, and she's not as good-looking as some of the other entrants."

Suddenly a girl's voice came on the line and it wasn't Jade. "Oh, and I suppose *you* are?" she said.

"Who's that?" I asked, thinking it might be

Tamara who'd picked up the other line.

I heard Jade laugh. "It's Fizz, dummy. She's been listening on the extension the whole time."

I was aghast. "That's *really* mean, Jade."

I would never have said anything if I'd known Fizz was actually there. It was bad enough that Jade had it in for me, but another contestant hating me as well . . . that was *all* I needed.

I put the phone down and stared out of the window. Now what? I thought. What am I going to do? Nowhere to stay, no lift, and two contestants who would be more than glad if I didn't make it up there at all.

I picked up the phone again and dialed Elliott's number. Maybe I could stay with him.

"'Fraid not," he said after I'd filled him in. "The whole family is down this time, to do the post-Christmas sales. Don't you know anyone else? You must know someone in London. You *can't* not come."

I racked my brains after I'd put down the phone. Who? Then a thought struck me. Ollie went to school up there. Maybe I could sneak into his dorm and sleep under his bed. But no, he was away on his skiing trip and his school would be closed. Maybe Lia's sister. Would Star be back from her holiday in Bermuda? My hopes rose again and I picked up the phone to dial Lia's number.

Half an hour later, it was all sorted again. Phew. Lia's dad was going to drive up to London as he wanted to see Star, and even better, Lia was going to come as well. Once again I thought, Never, never, never give up.

Staying at Star's was the best thing ever. Her flat is exactly how I want mine to be when I leave home. It's on the first floor of an old house in Notting Hill Gate and although it's tiny, it's mega-glamorous, like walking into a luxurious sheik's tent. She'd painted it all soft lavender and cornflower blue, and there were gorgeous Indian fabrics everywhere—soft muslins at the windows, silk cushions, and throws. And on every wall were framed magazine covers with pictures of Star. She's worked as a model for all the glossies and is absolutely stunning. Like the rest of her family, she has a perfect heart-shaped face and amazing cheekbones—only her hair is cut short and spiky, unlike Lia's.

She made me feel really welcome. We sent out for Japanese food, including sushi, then drank mint tea. I felt really grown-up and glam sitting with her in her living room.

In the evening, Mr. Axford went off to stay with one of his rock-band friends and Star wanted to have a girlie night in. She insisted on dressing me for the competition, even though I told her that the stylists were supposed to be coming in to dress the final ten contestants. "That's if I get through," I said. "There's fifteen boys and fifteen girls left, but it will be down to ten of each by lunchtime tomorrow."

"Oh, you'll get through," she said. "A gorgeous girl like you."

I was dead chuffed with the compliment, especially as she was a model and Lia had told me that Star never gives false praise.

"But don't wait for the stylists," Star went on. "They don't always know what suits you best, believe me—I've worked with enough of them. No, best to go with some idea of how you want to look or else they might put you in something you feel weird in. That can knock your confidence."

She went into her bedroom and came back with a pile of amazing clothes that she'd been given on her photo shoots, and Lia and I had a great night trying everything on and doing our hair and nails. When we settled down on the sofa bed later, I couldn't sleep. I felt so happy, like a whole new world was opening up for me. So much had happened over the last few weeks. I'd met some brilliant people and now was staying in probably the most fabtastic flat in London. It was loads better than it would have been camping on the floor in two-faced Jade's bedroom. It made me think about how things don't always turn out the way you expect them to, but if you don't give up trying, then sometimes they can work out even better than you imagined. I must remember to tell Dad, I thought. He's obviously forgotten.

Round Three

15

ELLIOTT DID a long wolf-whistle when he saw me the next day. He was sitting on the steps outside the hall with a number of the other contestants waiting to go in. Jade and Fizz were there too, and Jade looked surprised when she saw me. She whispered something to Fizz, who laughed. I decided that I wasn't going to stoop to their level so I purposely walked near them and smiled.

"Hi," I said.

They both looked at me as though I was a bad smell under their noses, then turned away. Fine, I thought, be like that, and I went to sit with Elliott.

"You look great," he said. "Very rock chick."

"Thanks," I replied. I did feel great, despite Jade and Fizz. Star had lent me some top clothes—black Gucci jeans, which fitted like a dream, a handkerchief top, and the most amazing black leather jacket by someone called Joseph. I felt a million dollars and ready for anything.

"So, all set for today?"

"Just about," I said.

"What song are you doing?"

"'Endless Love.' What about your lot? Do you think the winner stands out yet?"

He shrugged. "I ought to say, Yes, *me*, but who knows? There are a few lads in there who are major-league talent."

"Same in our group," I said. "I think just about everyone still in deserves to win."

A moment later, the doors opened and, as we all got up to go in, I spotted the television cameras inside the reception area and felt a rush of adrenalin.

"Do the nerves *ever* go away?" I asked Elliott.

"Doubt it," he said. "But nerves are supposed to be good. They say that the day you don't have them, is the day you lose your edge."

"Oh good," I said, "because my knees have just gone to jelly."

Elliott grinned. "You'll be okay. And good luck."

"Yeah, like, break a leg," sneered Jade as she walked past.

What is her problem? I asked myself as I followed her in. I've never done anything to her.

This time, all the girls and boys had to wait together in a small hall until we were called. One by one we were called in and Sushila was first up.

She gave me a smile when she came out and came over to sit with Elliott and me. Jade looked really peeved. I knew she was dying to know what went on, but she couldn't bring herself to come over.

"How did it go?" I asked.

"Okay, I think. The cameras are in there, which is a bit unnerving, but I think I was okay."

"And how were the judges?" asked Elliott.

"Not giving anything away," said Sushila. "Like stone statues. Very encouraging. Not."

I was called in fifth and I made sure I walked in confidently and gave the judges a big smile.

"Okay," said Sarah. "When you're ready."

I started singing, and Martin Riley stopped me about a quarter of the way through. "Okay, Becca, now start again, but this time do it with more conviction."

"Okay," I said, determined not to let him

unnerve me. I thought I had done it with conviction, but anyway . . . I started again.

"No," said Martin, interrupting again. "Now you're trying too hard. Take it back a bit. It's an emotional song so don't just belt it out."

I know what you're doing, I thought. You're testing to see if I'm going to crack. Well, I'm not. I started again, and this time, he let me finish. I think I did as well as I could do—I sang in tune and tried to inject as much feeling as possible. When I finished, I glanced over at the judges. Paul and Martin were looking down at their writing pads, and Paul was writing something, but at least Sarah gave me a smile.

"Okay, Becca," she said. "Not long to wait this time as there's only thirty of you to see. We'll let you know at lunchtime if you're going through."

And then it was back to the waiting. I sat and chatted to Sushila while the others went in. She was really nice. It was good to know that I had one ally in the girl's group. One dark-haired girl called Olivia looked a bit shaken when she came out and went and sat in the corner, looking a bit lost. I decided to go and talk to her as I remembered how I'd felt when Cat was voted out and how lonely it can be.

"Hey," I said, sitting next to her.

"Hey," she said.

"How was it in there?"

"Awful," she said. "I don't think I'm through."

I decided to share my newfound wisdom with her. "You don't know that. It's not over until it's over," I said. "Thing is, we mustn't give up. My dad's taught me that. Keep trying. He says the cream always rises to the top of the milk eventually. Same if you have talent. It will win through. And we've got this far—that must say something."

"God, you're so positive," she said. "But really, I don't think I was very good today."

"Ah," I said. "But everyone feels the same. That's what you have to remember. We're all feeling nervous and have had our confidence knocked a bit. So we're all up against the same stuff."

"I guess," she said, then smiled. "Yeah. It's not the end of the world is it?"

"Nah," I said. "We're only fourteen. This has

been the most brilliant experience and it's not even over yet. Look at us, in the last fifteen girls and that's out of thousands."

"Yeah." She smiled. "That is something, isn't it? I guess that I've been so intent on getting through today that I hadn't even thought about how far we've come."

"Exactly," I said.

The judges finished seeing everyone at about half past one and then Tanya divided us into three groups of ten, mixing girls with boys.

"Eek," said Sushila, who was put in a group with Jade, Fizz, and Elliott. "Know what this means, don't you? One of the groups is out and that will leave the final twenty."

"Oh God," I said, feeling *another* rush of nerves and wishing I was with Elliott and Sushila. "I hope I'm through."

"You will be, Becca," said Sushila, looking over at the third group. "I reckon that group over there won't make it. See that guy with the blond crew cut? I can tell you he wasn't good when I heard him, so don't worry, I reckon your group is a goer."

Tanya called for everyone's attention, then asked Jade's group to stay where they were. After that, she led the remaining twenty of us into the corridor, then put ten in one room and the other ten in a second room.

"Here we go again," I groaned to Olivia, who was in my group. "I can't bear this tension."

"I know," she said. "And it doesn't help with the cameras in the corridor, watching every expression."

"I know," I said. "You can almost feel them cheering inside when they catch someone crying. My mate Squidge says they love it when someone breaks down as it makes good telly."

After Tanya had left us, everyone was very quiet, straining to hear what was going on in the other rooms and waiting for the sound of footsteps. Every time we heard anyone walk past, everyone looked up expectantly, then when they didn't come in, people's shoulders would drop and it was back to waiting. After about ten minutes of excruciating silence, we heard a huge cheer from the room next door.

"One lot through, then," said Olivia. "Fingers crossed for us."

Five minutes later, the doors opened and a cameraman came through and started filming our group.

"Come to catch the tears of success or failure," said Olivia.

Sarah and Paul came through the door after the cameraman.

"Sorry to keep you waiting like this, everyone," Paul said, "as I know you're all eager to hear what's happening. First, I'd like to say how brilliant you've all been. . . ."

He doesn't need to say any more, I said to myself as he went on saying how good everyone had been. I know the dumping-you speech—the "I'd like to say how much I like you and I hope we can stay friends et cetera, et cetera" speech. Anyone with half a brain knows what it means.

"So," Paul went on, "I'm afraid we won't be asking you to go through to the next round. But don't be too disappointed. You've all done brilliantly to have come this far, and I hope to be seeing some of you again in future competitions."

Blah, blah, I thought. Dumped.

Chocfest Blues

16

LIA AND Star were lovely when I got back to the flat on Saturday afternoon. Star told me there would be other chances and that I could go and stay with her whenever I wanted. She even gave me her Gucci jeans, because, she said, they looked so good on me. I hardly took in anything they said. I just felt numb.

"I don't get every job I'm up for," Star said the next day as we were getting ready for her dad to come and pick us up, "but you soon learn in the modeling business that you have to take it on the chin—not take it personally, get on with the next thing. You'll get there in the end, Becca."

And Mr. Axford was so sweet on the journey back home. "It's a tough business," he said. "You win some and you lose some. You mustn't give up. I had my share of setbacks in the early days, believe you me."

Seems like everyone has their stories to tell, I

thought as I sat in the back and stared out the window, but it's different when it happens to you. I don't know if I want to be involved in a business that knocks your confidence all the time.

Dad gave me a big hug when I got home, and Mum bustled about making cups of tea, like that was going to help. In fact people being nice to me only made me feel worse, like I was ill or something and had to be treated with kid gloves. I wasn't ill. I wasn't anything. I felt numb. Deflated. Disappointed.

"You were so right, Dad," I said as I sipped my tea.

"About what?"

"To give up on your dream and go out and get a proper job," I said. "Save yourself a lot of pain."

"Oh, Becca," he said. "There'll be other chances for me *and* for you. And I haven't given up. I'll still be working on my book in the evenings and weekends."

Mum stood behind Dad and put her hands on his shoulders. "Your dad will get there in the end," she said. "But in the meantime, we have bills to pay. You have to be practical as well as have a dream."

"Well my dream's become a nightmare," I said.

Suddenly it was all too much, sitting there, chatting like the competition was in the distant past. I felt exhausted and I knew I was going to cry. I just wanted to get away, escape my parents' sympathetic looks and words of concern and consolation. I went upstairs and locked my bedroom door.

There was only one thing for it. Only one thing that would take away the pain . . . I rolled my desk chair over to the wardrobe, climbed onto it, and hauled down the box I'd put away at Christmas. Chocolates. Five whole boxes of chocolates. I opened the first box and scoffed them down like I hadn't eaten for weeks. Actually, I realized, I hardly had. All that stupid dieting, and for what? What was the point? All that stupid stuff I'd told myself about never giving up. Idiotic. You put in all your best effort and where does it get you? Nowhere.

After ten minutes I decided I needed something more. I unlocked the door, sneaked downstairs, and found the can of squirty cream Mum kept for special occasions and took it back upstairs. I put a squirt on every one of the chocolates and ate them, one after the other. Huh, I thought as I swallowed a toffee cream, that's to spite you, stupid Martin Riley. You had it in for me from Day One. Then I ate a hazelnut crunch. And that's for you, Jade Macey, who's got through to the next round with her ugly friend Fizz. Next was a strawberry cream, not my favorite, but topped with an extra squirt of cream—down it went, to spite *all* of them. I hate life, I thought as I went for gold and crammed in two chocolates at the same time. Just when you think everything's going your way, a great big bulldozer comes along and flattens you. I hate myself, I thought, for being so stupid, so full of myself. I winced when I remembered how I'd pratted around, giving everyone "good advice." They must have thought I was a right plonker, I thought. Fat lot of good it did anyone. And I hate school and it stinking well starts tomorrow and everyone will be gossiping. Oh, there's that Rebecca Howard. She thought she was it, you know. Thought she had the makings of a Pop Princess, stupid idiot. We knew she'd never make it. What ever made her think she would?

Oh God. I have no future, no life, no hope.

After I'd finished three-quarters of the second box of chocs, I started to feel very strange. I groaned and lay back on my bed. Then there was a knock on my door.

"Are you in there, Becca?" asked Dad.

"No," I said. "Leave me alone. I don't want to talk to anyone." I certainly didn't want to talk to Dad anymore. It was *his* stupid fault I'd got so carried away, putting all those daft ideas into my head about never giving up. What a load of rubbish. If I hadn't listened to him, I wouldn't have had to go through all this. And I wouldn't be feeling so sick now.

"Cat's on the phone."

"Tell her I've gone to Katmandu with the milk-man," I said. I didn't even want to talk to her. There was nothing she could say. Although to give her her due, she had tried. They all had. As soon as I'd got back to Star's flat, the phone had started going—Cat, Squidge, and Mac, all wanting to know how it had gone.

Mac. Stupid git. I didn't even know if he was my boyfriend anymore. We hadn't been out on a date in ages and we hadn't snogged each other properly for weeks. Maybe it was all over and I'd been so wrapped up I hadn't noticed I'd been dumped by him as well as the competition.

Squidge. Stupid git. It was really all *his* fault. Him and that stupid dare. It was all right for all of them. They'd done it for a laugh. Squidge told me that Andy Warhol once said that everyone has their fifteen minutes of fame. The Pop Princess competition was mine. And now it was over. Forever.

But Mac is the *stupidest* git, thinking I was off with Elliott all the time. As if a boy like him would ever take an interest in me. He probably felt sorry for me.

And Cat, well, she's just a stupid git, because . . . because everyone is, especially me. I'm the most stupid git of all, stupid, stupid, *stupid*.

I felt tears pricking the back of my eyes again. And now I'm going to cry, I thought as tears started to spill down my cheeks. And I don't care. I am a loser, a failure. A stupid, stupid person. Then there was a sudden lurch in my stomach and, oops, better run for it. I'm going to . . . eeeew . . .

As I kneeled on the bathroom floor, I caught sight of my reflection in the mirror—mad hair, red eyes, deathly white, and on my knees with chocolate smeared around my mouth. "Hey, Pop Princess," I said as I grimaced at myself. "This is what happens when you try to exceed your grasp or whatever that stupid quote of Dad's is." To have imagined I could have actually won Pop Princess. Hah. Never again. Never, never, never, never, never, never, never . . .

I went back into my bedroom and lay on the bed, ready for another good cry. Once again, there was a knock at the door.

"Becca," said Mum.

"Go away," I called. "I need to be alone."

"Okay," said Mum. "It's just that someone from the competition is on the phone for you."

"Who?" I said. "Elliott?" I'd already spoken to Elliott on Saturday after the "dumping." He was lovely. He'd put his arm around me and hadn't come out with any of the clichés about trying again or getting another chance, et cetera. He just held me tight, like he understood.

"No," said Mum through the door. "It's someone called Martin Riley."

I sat up like a shot. Martin Riley? Ohmigod, I

thought. What does he want? . . . Probably phoned to check I haven't put my head in a gas oven. Probably checking that I'm okay. I don't know if I want to hear him come out with some claptrap about being a good loser.

But my curiosity had been aroused. It couldn't hurt to just hear what he had to say. . . .

"Are you going to pick up your phone?" asked Mum. "Or shall I ask him to call back later?"

"No, no," I said as I smoothed my hair and wiped away chocolate smears. "I'll take it."

I picked up the phone. "Er, hello?"

"Becca," said Martin. "Sorry to call so late, but we needed to get in touch with you."

I didn't say anything.

"So you got home okay?" he asked.

D'oh, *obviously*, I thought. "Yes, thank you," I said.

"Have you been crying, Becca?" he asked. "Your voice sounds a bit funny."

"Um, no," I said. "Bit bunged up, that's all. Um, hayfever."

"Ah," said Martin. "Yes, hayfever. I always get

hayfever in January. Anyway, I may have a cure for you. Reason I'm calling is, we've had a problem with one of the finalists, Fiona McPhilbin—I think you all know her as Fizz? Well, she lied about her age. Remember the entry age was up to sixteen? Well she was seventeen at the beginning of December and so we've had no choice but to disqualify her."

My head started to spin. Why was he telling *me*? What did it mean?

"So Sarah, Paul, and I put our heads together," he continued, "and decided that we'd like to ask you to come back. It was very close between you and another contestant anyway. I don't think you knew that. So, what do you say? Give it another shot?"

17

The Final

PROGRAM FOR POP PRINCE
AND POP PRINCESS FINAL

Saturday, January 11th — Starts 4:00 p.m.

Pop Princes

1) Jason Barker: "Bridge Over Troubled Water" (Simon and Garfunkel)
2) Mark Bosman: "Everything I Do (I Do It For You)" (Bryan Adams)
3) Ewan Hughes: "Candle in the Wind" (Elton John)
4) David Keenan: "Careless Whisper" (George Michael)
5) Scott Lewis: "Every Breath You Take" (Police)
6) Martin McDonnell: "Rock DJ" (Robbie Williams)
7) Jonathan McKeever: "You've Lost That Loving Feeling" (Righteous Brothers)
8) Paul Nash: "Waterloo Sunset" (The Kinks)
9) Rick Schneider: "I'm Not in Love" (10 CC)
10) Elliott Williams: "Suspicious Minds" (Elvis Presley)

Pop Princesses

1) Kate Anderson: "Turn to You" (Melanie C)
2) Charlotte Bennie: "Like a Prayer" (Madonna)
3) Jessica Harris: "Baby One More Time" (Britney Spears)
4) Becca Howard: "Nothing Compares 2 U" (Sinead O'Connor)
5) Alice Seymour Jones: "I Will Always Love You" (Whitney Houston)
6) Jade Macey: "My Heart Will Go On" (Celine Dion)
7) Heather Nicholson: "Can't Get You Out of My Head" (Kylie Minogue)
8) Marie Oliver: "Eternal Flame" (The Bangles)
9) Sushila Patel: "Hero" (Mariah Carey)
10) Chloe Wilson: "I Will Survive" (Gloria Gayner)

The final will be televised live and tickets will be available for friends and family. Please refrain from taking photographs during the performances. Thank you for your cooperation.

WHAT A top week. I phoned Cat, Squidge, Mac, and Lia immediately and told them the latest news. They went wild, like it was happening to them. But the best bit of the week was bumping in to Jade at school and seeing her face. She looked like I'd looked after my chocfest. Classmates were fantastic. Of course news had spread that I'd been out then in again, and I was amazed at the support I was given from everyone. Even people I didn't know. Even Jonno Appleton in Year Eleven.

Everyone came up to London for the final, as they were letting friends and family in to see the last performances. Mum and Dad stayed in a B&B around the corner from Star's. Cat, Lia, and I slept at Star's, and Squidge stayed with Mac at Mr. Macey's. I'd gone up on the Friday and had spent the Friday night and all day Saturday going over my song with a voice coach and a guy accompanying on the piano. They were totally brilliant and gave me some excellent tips. Late on Saturday afternoon, a stylist came in for a session with all the contestants, but I wasn't that bothered with what she had to say because I had my own personal stylist back at the flat—Star Axford and her wardrobe of fantastic designer clothes. When I dashed back to the flat just before the final show, I found that Star had picked out a stunning dress for me to wear. It was royal blue—not a color I'd normally choose, but it was low-cut, with a slit up the side and looked amazing with the pair of Jimmy Choo heels that she also lent me. She blow-dried my hair straight and loose and put the dress in a plastic carrier for me to change into when I got to the hall.

I felt so calm. It was weird, but having thought I'd lost once and then to be given a second chance, I had no expectations, and as Mum always says, Blessed is she who has no expectations, for she is never disappointed. I was lucky to be going at all, and I knew it.

Loads of press were waiting outside the hall when we arrived and one of them called over to Lia.

"Hey, you one of the finalists?"

"No," she replied, then pointed at me. "But my mate Becca is."

Suddenly I had a crowd buzzing around me and a

bunch of photographers snapping pictures.

"So how's it been? What do you think of your chances?"

"What's the atmosphere been like? Any nastiness between the contestants?"

"How do you see your future?"

"Just say 'no comment,'" whispered Cat.

"Er, it's been fantastic," I said. "All the contestants have been great. We're all very supportive of each other. Um. Don't know about my chances—everybody's really good."

Then we made a dash for the hall as the press swirled around one of the boy contestants who'd just walked in.

"God, this is so glamorous," said Cat when we got inside. "It's like you're a real star."

"I know. It's amazing, isn't it?" I said. It felt like a dream come true.

Mum and Dad were waiting in the foyer and I gave them a wave.

"Just do your best, love," said Dad, walking toward us. "We'll be out there with our fingers crossed for you."

Mum gave me a hug. "My little girl," she said. "I'm so proud of you."

"Thanks, Mum. Anyway, got to go and get ready."

Elliott arrived a moment later, ran over, and gave me a huge hug. "How top is this?" he said. "Both of us in the finals. You said it's never over until it's over and you were right."

I gave him a huge hug back. "I know. I still can hardly believe I'm here."

He took my hand and led me toward the performers' door. Of course that had to be the exact moment that Mac arrived with Squidge, who was holding a kid I'd never seen before by the hand. I saw Mac's face light up when he saw me, then shut down when he saw Elliott holding my hand. It was awful.

Right, Mac Macey, I thought. I'm going to deal with you *this* instant. Being dumped from the competition made me do a lot of thinking, and a lot of it was about Mac. I'd neglected him horribly at a time when he really needed me—a time when you turn to your mates and hope they'll be there for you. I hadn't been there for him, because I'd been sitting on my Pop Princess cloud. But the semifinal had brought me down to Earth with a thump, and boy was I glad I had my mates. Even though I hadn't wanted to talk to them at first, I *had* appreciated just how supportive they'd been through all of it, even Mac. He'd sorted it out so that I could stay with his dad, Lia had sorted it so that I could stay with Star, Cat and Squidge had listened to all my rehearsals and had been encouraging every time. Cat and Squidge and Lia had been totally top and not at all critical that I'd only been thinking about myself for the last few weeks.

I pulled Elliott over to Squidge and Mac.

"This is Elliott," I said to the boys. "He's been my best mate in the competition and I reckon he's going to win."

Elliott smiled and shrugged. "I wish."

Squidge said, "Hi," and Mac sort of mumbled.

"Elliott," I continued, "these are my best mates from home. Squidge and my *boyfriend,* Mac."

I let go of Elliott's hand, took Mac's, and gave him a big smacker on the cheek. "We've been going out for about . . . how long has it been, Mac?"

Mac squeezed my hand and smiled. "About three months . . ." Then he laughed. "And one week, three days, nine hours . . ."

Elliott laughed. "You're a lucky bloke, mate. You make sure you hang on to her."

"Oh, I will." Mac grinned at me. "I *will*."

I looked over at the little girl who had been holding on to Squidge's hand through all this. She looked about eight—a bit young, even for Squidge. "And who's your new girlfriend, Squidge?" I teased.

"This is Tamara," said Mac. "Sonia's daughter. She wouldn't let us come without her, would you, T?"

Tamara smiled up at Mac like they were oldest, bestest friends. "Not after I heard that Mac's girlfriend was in the competition," she said, blushing.

"Yes . . . and I just need to have a private moment with him," I said, and took him aside. "So, how's it going? At the flat. You know, with Sonia and her daughter and stuff?" This was something I'd promised myself I'd do from now on—take an interest in what was happening to him, even if there was something happening to me as well.

Mac smiled. "Okay . . . Tamara's cool. She's a kid." Then he grinned. "In fact I think she's got a bit of a crush on Squidge. She asked if he had a girlfriend. I think she wants to marry him when she grows up."

"And what about Sonia?"

"Okay too. We get on all right, I guess," said Mac. "She's okay. And Dad does seem happier. I had a chat with him and he's not going to move in with her or anything. And he said she's not going to be there every time I go up. So yeah, I guess it might be okay."

"It *will* be okay," I said as I took his hand. "And I wanted to say I'm sorry I've been such a pain all these weeks. You know, like totally self-obsessed."

Mac squeezed my hand. "Hey, no biggie. I'm sorry *I've* been such a pain. I could have been more supportive. I guess I got a bit jealous. I dunno; it felt like I was losing you or something."

"I think I lost myself back there for a while. But after tonight, it's all back to normal," I said.

Elliott came over and looked at his watch. "Show-time, folks."

Mac put his arms around me and gave me a huge bear hug. "Good luck, kiddo. Now go and show them what you can do."

Happy, happy, happy, I thought as I headed for the dressing room. And here I go again. But this time it felt so different, in a really good way.

After we'd got ready, the girl contestants were allowed to sit in the audience with the others to watch the boys. My dad's eyes almost fell out of their sockets when he saw me walk in wearing Star's dress. I thought it was a good job I was sitting in a different section as he'd probably have made me go and change into something less revealing. Too late, Dad. Chances to dress like this don't come around very often and it wasn't as though I was out of place in my designer frock. All the contestants had really pulled out the stops and looked amazing. I was used to seeing everyone in their jeans and trainers, but now we all looked like we'd just stepped on to the red carpet at the Oscars.

The lights went down and Paul Parker walked onto the stage. He explained how the voting worked and what time the lines would close for each category. Then he began to introduce the male contestants. It was fantastic to sit there and watch them all. The girls hadn't had a chance to see what the boys had been up to because we'd always been in a separate hall. As each of them sang, I thought they were all really good, but of course, I was rooting for Elliott. I couldn't wait to hear him perform.

The audience cheered like mad after every performance. It was really obvious where the friends and family of each contestant were sitting as they went wild when their boy was up. Elliott was on last and when Paul announced his name and he walked out to center stage I felt my stomach tighten with nerves on his behalf. He looked every inch a Pop Prince in black leather trousers, a black T-shirt, and with spiked hair. It was clear he worked out as well, as he had great muscle tone. He'd even put some temporary tattoos on his arm to give him that "Robbie Williams" look. The music struck up and he sang "Suspicious Minds" by Elvis Presley. I thought, I might be biased, but he was easily the best. Confident, cheeky, and he had a great voice. I felt so chuffed for him at the end when the audience cheered madly, and I turned to see my mates, including Mac, standing and whistling with the others.

Before I knew it, Tanya was beckoning for the girls to go backstage. Shame, as I'd have loved to stay where I was and watch the other girls.

"You can wait here," said Tanya as she led us behind the curtains. "You won't be able to see, but you will be able to hear. Okay, Kate, you're on first, so stand over there. And good luck to all of you. You all look fabulous."

I stood with Sushila as Kate got ready for her name to be announced. Suddenly my newfound calm deserted me and my knees started to go. Ohmigod, I thought, it'll be me in a moment. Live on television, in front of thousands of viewers. It's not just three judges anymore, it's *thousands*. Ohmigod, ohmigod, ohmigod. Nervous, nervous, nervous.

Everything went into slow motion. Kate did her number, then Charlotte, then Jessica, and before I knew it, I heard Paul's voice saying, "And our next performer is Becca Howard from St. Antony, Cornwall. She's going to be singing 'Nothing Compares 2 U.'"

Sushila pushed me forward. "You're on. Good luck!"

My legs had turned from jelly to stone. "I can't move," I moaned.

Sushila pushed me again. "Yes you can, go *on*."

I took a deep breath and did a quick shake and tremble as Zac had taught me, then I walked out on to the stage and toward the microphone.

The spotlights were blinding. It all felt so unreal. Just breathe, Becca, I told myself. It's going to be okay. Oh God, please don't let me fall over or dry up or forget the words—please, please, please. I'd never felt so petrified. I looked at the audience and tried to find Mum and Dad and my mates. And there they were, all looking at me with so much hope and anticipation on their faces that I felt myself start to smile.

The music started up and I began to sing the opening lines. Suddenly I got an amazing rush. Here I was, singing in front of an audience, cameras on me, my friends and family in the audience . . .

This was my moment. It was going to be all right.

When I'd finished, the audience erupted into cheers and applause and I looked over to my support group. They were standing and clapping and whistling. It was so totally brilliant. And I swear I saw my mum put a handkerchief to her eye, like she was crying.

After that, it was over, and the next one was on. At last I could enjoy the rest of the performances. I'd done my bit and I could relax. From now on, it was up to the audience at home to phone in and decide on the winner.

When everyone had finished, there was a break for the guests to go and have refreshments while the contestants were led into a green room to wait for the public's verdict. The atmosphere was bubbling, not like the other times—this was *it* and we all knew it. I felt on top of the world and I buzzed about, telling everyone how brilliant they'd been and how great they looked. I even tried to congratulate Jade, but she did her usual snooty look, then turned away to talk to one of the guys, so I decided not to bother. Why ruin the atmosphere with one of her snide comments, I thought. I'd done what I could with her and she was still being off with me so why waste energy? I didn't need her to like me. Why had I been so bothered about making someone I didn't even like, like me? I had enough real friends without her.

About half an hour later we were all called back onto the stage and the guests took their seats once more.

"The phone lines for Pop Prince have now closed and the votes have been counted," said Martin. "But before we announce our winners, I should say that I and the other two judges have been extremely impressed by the standard of the contestants. They've worked hard and taken a lot of criticism, mainly from me. But they've stuck it out and I'd like to stress that all the contestants here are winners tonight."

"Blah, blah," I said, and grinned at Sushila, who grinned back.

"So, without further ado, I'll pass the microphone over to Sarah, who holds the results for our Pop

Prince," Martin said. "Let's see how the public voted. Over to you, Sarah."

Sarah took the microphone. "In third place," she announced, "with eighteen percent of the vote, we have . . . Martin McDonnell."

The audience cheered madly as Martin stepped forward and stood beside her.

"In second place, with twenty-two percent of the vote . . . Ewan Hughes."

More cheering and I glanced over at Elliott. He smiled at me and gulped, so I held up my hands to show that my fingers were crossed for him.

"And finally, this year's Pop Prince, with thirty-eight percent of the votes . . ."

Dead silence.

". . . Elliott Williams."

Elliott gasped, went bright red, then stepped forward to shake Sarah's hand. The audience went wild. I glanced back at the seven boys who hadn't been chosen. I really felt for them as they must have been terribly disappointed, but they were all doing their best to keep smiling and look happy for Elliott.

Once the awards had been given and photos taken

of the three boys, Sarah took the microphone again. "And now, we finally get to our Pop Princesses. Tanya can you bring out the results please?"

I felt all ten of us stiffen in anticipation as Tanya walked over to Sarah. Who would it be?

Tanya seemed to whisper something in Sarah's ear, then Sarah nodded and turned to the audience.

"I'm sorry," she said into the microphone, "but there will be a slight delay in announcing the winner. The technicians are having problems with a couple of the phone lines and people haven't been getting through. Perhaps while we're waiting, we could ask our Pop Prince to come forward and sing for us again. I'll keep you informed and let you know as soon as we have some news."

"Oh argghhh," said Sushila, leaning against me.

"I know," I said. "Argh, argh, *argh* . . ."

Duchess

18

THE MORNING after we got back from London, I had a lie-in until eleven o'clock. Mum said that even though it was a bit naughty, I could have the morning off school. She and Dad were even taking time off. It felt like bliss to sleep in and not have to think about songs or rehearsals or what I'd wear or losing half a stone. Bliss, bliss, bliss.

When I finally got up and went down to breakfast, I found Dad grinning and waving an envelope at me.

"What?" I asked.

"Good news," he said. "Nothing definite yet, but it's a step in the right direction. It's a letter from an agent. A very good agent in London. She likes the outline and chapters I sent her and wants to see the rest of the book."

"So does that mean you'll have a deal?" I asked.

"No," said Dad, "but it means someone is taking

me seriously. These guys don't waste time if they're not really interested. If she takes me on, she'll try and get me a deal. So fingers crossed for me, Becca."

"So will you give up your job?" I asked. Although I was glad he had received a positive response, I didn't want to go back to those nights lying awake listening to him and Mum arguing.

"No, I won't give up the job," he said. "In fact I'm beginning to enjoy it. I missed being in a working environment, missed the stimulation. I'd only give up work if I made it on to the best-seller lists and stayed there for the better part of a year. I can write *and* work for the time being."

"That's fantastic, Dad," I said. "You deserve a break."

"Too right," said Mum, coming in through the back door with a carrier bag. "I'm going to cook your dad a celebratory breakfast. Scrambled eggs, smoked salmon, and"——she pulled out a bottle of champagne——"a bit of bubbly."

Dad looked really chuffed. "Oh, Megan, you needn't have . . ."

"No bother," she said, and kissed the top of his

head. "I think it's important to celebrate the small successes in life as well as the big ones. And Lord knows, you've tried hard enough to get someone to pay you some attention. And of course, there's Becca's news. . . ."

Mum put the champagne in an ice bucket, then found three glasses.

"Who else is coming?" I asked.

"It's for you, you daft ninny," she said, then she popped the cork and poured three glasses. "You can have it with some orange juice."

I took the glass she offered me and held it up the way people do at weddings. "A toast," I said. "To my dad, the famous novelist."

Dad lifted his glass. "To my lovely family, without whom none of it means anything."

"So you're not going to split up, then?" I asked.

Mum looked shocked. "*Split up?* Of course not!"

"Whatever made you think that, Becca?" asked Dad.

I shrugged. "Nothing. Just heard you rowing sometimes."

"All couples row sometimes, love," said Mum. "It

doesn't mean they don't love each other."

"You've not been worried about this for long, have you?" asked Dad.

"No . . . yeah, sort of. People *do* break up, you know," I said. "Like Mac's mum and dad."

"Well, you don't need to worry about us," said Dad. "We're in for the duration. It would take a lot more than a few rows to break us up."

Mum raised her glass. "To us," she said. "Our little family. To you, Joe—wishing you every success. And to you, Becca—singer extraordinaire and our very own Pop Duchess."

"Duchess?" I asked.

"Well, that lovely Indian girl won the title Pop Princess. You came third, so I reckon that makes you a Duchess."

I laughed and gave a royal wave. "It was top, wasn't it?"

"I've never felt so proud of you," said Mum. "You were brilliant."

It had been brilliant. We only had to wait half an hour for the phones to start working again then the results came through. Sushila won, with thirty-five percent of the vote, Jade came in second with twenty-one percent of the votes, then . . . me. *Me!* With nineteen percent of the votes. I was over the moon. Delirious. Ecstatic. Sushila deserved to win—she stood out a mile. And Jade—well, I've always known Jade was good. She wasn't too happy about coming second, though, and couldn't help showing it. Shame, because when the press pictures come, everyone's going to see what a sulky cow she really is.

I was gobsmacked that I came third. I really, really, *really* didn't expect it. I was hoping for sixth or seventh or something, so coming in third had far exceeded my expectations.

After a lovely morning with my parents, I finally got into school at lunchtime. Everyone in the playground cheered. It was fantastic. Loads of people came up and said, "Well done" and "You were fab" and "We saw you on telly" . . . I felt like a real star. The press had put our school on the map for having two competitors in the finals. One paper said there must be something in the Cornish air that breeds talent. That should keep my teachers happy, I thought. Maybe they'll give me a better report next time.

As we were going into classes for the afternoon, Miss Segal waved for me to go over to her.

"Yes, Miss Segal," I said.

"Well first, I believe congratulations are in order," she said. "I saw you and Jade last night. You were both fantastic. I felt so proud. That's why I wanted to have a word. It's about the Easter show. I don't know if you've noticed yet, but I put a notice up about it last week and I wondered if you'd like to take part this time."

I felt really chuffed. To actually be *asked* this time.

"Of course Jade will be wanting a leading role, but I'm sure there will be room for both of you," continued Miss Segal. "We're going to be casting next week. So what do you think? Would you like to be in it?"

I glanced over at Mac, who was standing behind her. "Um, yes, sort of, but I . . . I don't want a lead part. In fact I don't even really want to be in it."

Miss Segal looked puzzled. "So what would you like, then?"

"How about if I get involved in the other side of things—like producing?"

Miss Segal was obviously surprised. "Why produce and not sing?"

"Couple of things. First: I've been thinking a lot about what I want to do when I'm older. I could carry on with my singing, but most singers, unless they're Kylie or Madonna or someone, they only have a short time at the top, and then what? What would I do if that was me? It would be back to all the angst I felt throughout that competition."

Miss Segal smiled. "What a sensible girl you are, Becca. Most girls your age wouldn't have that kind of foresight. So what's the other reason?"

"Something Mac said to me ages ago. About managing and producing and the people who make it all happen. I think maybe I could go into producing or management when I'm older and the school show would be good practice to see if I'd like it."

"Well, yes. And I'm sure your experiences from

the show will stand you in good stead if you want to pursue producing. But that's my job, really."

"Maybe you could use an assistant? I think I learned a lot doing that competition, about people needing encouragement and ways to relax, as it can all be pretty stressful."

"It can indeed," said Miss Segal, looking closely at me. Then she smiled again. "This is a surprise, Becca. Very encouraging that you haven't got your head in the clouds and been carried away by it all."

"No," I said. "I've seen how good the competition is out there. It won't be an easy ride for anyone, not even Sushila or Elliott, who won first prize."

"So you'd rather be a big fish in a small pond?"

"For now, I guess," I said. "Until I know what I want to do. Then, well . . . you can achieve anything if you put your mind to it and work hard."

Miss Segal leaned back against the wall in mock shock. "I can't believe I'm hearing this," she said, laughing.

"And with the Easter show, could I be involved from the beginning—with the casting as well?"

Miss Segal nodded. "Yes, I don't see why not. You could sit in on that as well."

Fab, I thought. It would be interesting sitting on the other side of things, and I decided I wouldn't be mean to anyone, even if they were rotten. And I wouldn't be horrid to Jade, but I doubted she'd even want to be in it once she heard I was producing.

"And, um, you know what you just said about me being sensible and having foresight and stuff?"

"Yes, Becca?"

"Well, er, could you put that in my next report?"

Miss Segal laughed. "Yes, of course I can. How about this: Becca shows great ambition, but her head isn't in the clouds; in fact her feet are firmly planted on the ground and she seems to know exactly where she's going."

I beamed back at her. "Sounds excellent to me."

Don't miss the next round of
Truth or Dare!
Turn the page for an excerpt of . . .

Teen Queens
and
Has-Beens

Cathy Hopkins

Mystery Admirer?

EVERYONE was hanging out in the corridor by the assembly hall when I got in. All the talk was about the school Valentine's disco and cards, with lots of whispering, giggling, and secret looks as people tried to guess who'd sent which card to who and who'd left which card in whose locker or rucksack.

"So, how many did you get?" asked Becca.

"Oh, way too many to count," I replied, trying to laugh it off. I started to count on my fingers. "One from Robbie Williams, one from Matt Damon, one from Eminem . . ."

Becca's eyes widened. "Really?"

Cat punched her arm. "No, she's kidding you."

I laughed. Becca was so gullible. She thinks that because Dad's in the music business that we know everyone. "How many cards did you get, Bec?"

"Just one. I guess it's from Mac," said Becca as

she pulled her long red hair into a ponytail. "At least it better had be seeing as I sent him one. What about you, Cat?"

"One. Don't know who it's from. At first I thought it was from Squidge, as we've sent each other cards for years, but it's not his writing. I'd know his scrawl even if he tried to disguise it."

"I think people ought to sign Valentine's cards," said Becca. "It would save a lot of grief knowing who they were from."

"They do in some places," I said. "One of my mates at my old school was American and she said that sometimes they sign them there."

"Yeah, but it would take the mystery out it," said Cat. "It's fun trying to guess."

"Did you send Squidge a card?" I asked.

Cat shook her head. "It's not like that with us anymore."

"Did you send Ollie one?"

"Nah. I reckon his head's big enough as it is and no doubt he'll get a sack-load despite me. But seriously, Lia, how many did you get?"

I made my finger and thumb into an *O*.

"I don't get it," said Cat. "I mean, look at you. You're stunning, tall, long blond hair, silver-blue eyes . . . you're most boys' fantasy girl! Boys visibly dribble when you enter a room, and no, don't shake your head, I've seen them. By my reckoning, half the school is madly in love with you."

"Yeah, but some of the boys here like to act really hard," said Becca. "You know, they think that they'd look like soppy Sarahs if they did anything remotely romantic like send a card. Pathetic, isn't it? Doesn't mean that you haven't got loads of boys interested in you, though, Lia."

"So why haven't I had one single date since I got here, then?"

"Beneath the hard act, most boys are chickens," said Becca. "They're intimidated. You're beautiful, a five-star babe and most of them know that they're not in your league. Boys hate rejection more than anything, so I reckon most of them daren't ask you out for fear of being turned down."

"I agree," said Cat. "Anyway, you're not missing much. Our school isn't exactly Talent City."

Becca punched Cat's arm. "Er, excuse me. Mac?"

"Yeah, course," said Cat. "And Squidge, but I don't count them. They're mates."

I didn't say anything, but privately, I think I could fancy Squidge if I let myself. But I don't go there, seeing as Cat and he were an item for ages and they're still really close mates. I don't know how she'd feel about me being into Squidge and I don't want to mess up anything between us. So I'm happy to just be good friends with him. Besides, I don't think I'm his type. I'm tall and blond, and Cat is petite and dark, plus he's never given the slightest indication that he feels the same way about me.

"There's always Jonno Appleton," said Becca, glancing at a tall boy with spiky dark hair from Year Eleven, who was standing by the doors. "He's a nine out of ten in anybody's book."

"Yeah," I said, "I do fancy him, but who doesn't? Anyway, he's taken by Rosie Crawford, so it's hands off. Boyfriend stealing is against my rules."

"What do we care?" said Cat. "Isn't Ollie bringing that Michael guy down from London with him tonight?"

I felt my face flush. "Yeah. Michael Bradley."

"Does Ollie know that you like him?" asked Becca.

"No way," I said. "And you mustn't say anything. I'd die. No, I'd never tell Ollie, as he might think he could do me a favor or something and try and fix us up. No, I want it to happen naturally."

I've known Michael since I was knee-high and had a crush on him since I was seven. Not that he's ever noticed me, not in a big way. I'm just Ollie's kid sister, someone to thrash at tennis and throw in the swimming pool in summer. But tonight I intend to change all that. We haven't seen each other for nearly a year, and when Ollie told me that he was bringing him down for Mum's party, my imagination went into overdrive. My plan was to persuade Ollie to come with Michael to the school disco with the rest of us. That way, I could show Michael off a bit and prove to the school that I am not totally repulsive to boys. Then later at Mum's do . . . well, who knows what a romantic night in Venice might bring?

When the last bell went in the afternoon, school emptied in a flash. Doubtless everyone had their plans. Home, shower, dress, makeup, back to school. Our plan was to meet at Cat's, get dressed there, go to the school disco for an hour or so, then up to my house for Mum's latest extravaganza. She said that I could invite anyone I liked from school, but I'd only invited Becca, Cat, Squidge, and Mac.

It's funny, but since I came down here, sometimes I feel a bit awkward about how rich my family is. It's like I don't want anyone to think I'm showing off or flaunting it. All I've ever wanted was to be normal and be accepted and that was easy at my old school because most people's parents were loaded or famous. There was even a princess in Year Ten. Down here, though, people aren't as well off and sometimes all they see are the flash cars, the big house, and my dad's fame. What they don't know is that Mum and Dad lead very quiet lives most of the time. Both of them are real homebodies. Mum loves nothing better than pottering in the garden, growing herbs and vegetables, and Dad is happiest in his studio listening to sounds or watching the telly. But that's not what the public see. They see Dad on telly whenever he does interviews, which is rarely these days. Or in videos on MTV. They think that he's the wild man of rock and roll. The Cornish Ozzy Osbourne. I can't help being his daughter, and down here, I want to be Lia Axford—not Lia, Zac Axford, famous rock star's daughter. There's a difference, and sometimes it gets in the way of people's perception of me at my new school. I guess that's why I try to keep my family history quiet and in the background, so to speak.

I raced home to pick up my clothes to take to Cat's. It was complete pandemonium when I got there with even more people dashing about than there had been in the morning. The Venetian theme had really taken shape. A trio of musicians were rehearsing in the hall and there were ornate candelabras in the corridor leading to the right of the house where the marquee had been set up for the party. It's going to look really fab, I thought as I spotted Mum giving a group of caterers some last minute instructions.

"Is Ollie back?" I asked her.

She nodded her chin towards the stairs. "In his room with his friends, and oh, Lia, I'll leave a selection of masks in your room for you and your friends to put on when you're back from the school disco. Don't be back too late, okay?"

"Okay. Thanks, Mum," I said. Ollie's with his friends? Who else besides Michael, I wondered as I took the stairs two at a time. Never mind—the more, the merrier. I made a quick dash up to my room to brush my hair and spritz some Cristalle on before going to say hello and hopefully get Michael to notice me properly for the first time.

As soon as I opened my door, I noticed a blue envelope on my bed. My name had been written on it in beautiful handwriting. I ripped it open. It was a card with a red rose on it. Inside, it read: *To the girl with silver eyes, from a distant admirer who's waiting until the time is right to reveal himself. Happy Valentine's.* Then three kisses.

I felt a rush of excitement as I studied the envelope for clues. No stamp, so it must have been either delivered by hand or come from someone in the house.

Hmmm. Interesting, I thought as I heard Ollie and Michael's voices in the corridor outside.

Truth or Dare
Teen Queens and Has-Beens

AVAILABLE NOVEMBER 2004

* * *

The girls are back!

Turn the page for a sneak-peak of . . .

* * *

Mates, Dates and Mad Mistakes

by Cathy Hopkins

Chickens

"Sounds *horrible*," said Nesta, pulling a face.

"What?" I asked as Lucy and I came back into her bedroom with sleepover supplies (the usual: Diet Cokes, Salt & Vinegar Pringles, and Liquorice Allsorts). T. J., Nesta, and I were staying over at Lucy's, after she'd held a girls-only party earlier in the evening. We'd finished clearing up after the other girls had left and were ready for some late night nattering before getting into our sleeping bags.

"Yeah, what sounds horrible?" asked Lucy.

T. J. pointed to a book of spells that I'd lent Lucy earlier in the summer. "Becoming blood sisters," said T. J. in a spooky voice. "Says in Izzie's book that if you want to bond with your mates for life, the best way to do it is to each prick your finger with a needle, then press the tiny point of blood on your finger against the prick on your friends' fingers. It makes you sisters for life."

"Yee-uck," said Nesta. "Can't we burn our bras instead, like those women in the sixties?"

Lucy laughed. "No, we can't, because seeing as I have no chest to speak of, I haven't got a bra to burn."

"Yes, you have," said Nesta. "I've seen it."

Lucy shook her head. "I chucked it out. No point. It was after something Lal said. He asked, if I had no feet would I still wear shoes? I said no, course not. So then he said, so why do you wear a bra?"

"What a cheek. What does he know?" I said as I put down the Pringles. "That's really mean, even for a brother."

Lucy shrugged. "Nah, he's right. I only wore one because everyone else does. For show. Trouble was, nothing did show except an empty wrinkle of lacy fabric under my T-shirt. It's much more comfortable without one."

"Oh, let's do the blood sister thing," said T. J. "It'll be a laugh, and we'll be friends for ever and ever."

I shook my head. "Nah, sounds daft. It's the sort

of thing that kids do, junior school stuff. . . ."

"And this coming from Mystic Iz, Queen of Witchiness herself," said T. J. "What's up with you?"

I shrugged. "Nothing. It just sounds childish. I've had that spell book for years. I read it when I was in Year Seven."

T. J. looked disappointed. "I think it sounds cool. And there's a nice sentiment behind it-makes a change from all those spells you usually do for getting boys and stuff."

"Yeah, let's try it," said Lucy.

"Well, you have to sterilize the needles, you know," said Nesta.

Lucy rolled her eyes. "You're such a prissy-knickers."

"No, actually she's right," said T. J. "Best be on the safe side."

"Yes, better had, Lucy," I said. "T. J.'s parents are both doctors so if anyone should know about what's safe and what's not, it's them."

"Oh, all right," said Lucy. "I will."

"And as long as it won't hurt . . . ," said Nesta.

"It won't," said Lucy as she began to look for needles in her sewing box. She found a sachet of them and waved them in the air. "Won't be a mo. I'll just put on my nurse's uniform and go and sterilize these."

She was back a few minutes later and handed us a needle each.

"If we're going to do this, let's do it properly," I said. "We should sit in a circle, and, Lucy, can we light a candle?"

"Ah, so Mystic Iz isn't quite dead, then?" said Nesta, grinning.

Lucy found a candle, lit it, then turned off the electric light and we sat in a circle on the floor.

Lucy, T. J., and I did it straight away. A quick jab and we were ready.

Nesta screwed her face up and put the needle close to her thumb, like she was trying to puncture the skin really slowly. "I can't," she moaned. "I really can't. I hate needles, and it's going to hurt."

"Just do it quickly," said Lucy. "It just takes a second and only feels like . . . like a quick prick."

"I could answer that with something very rude,"

laughed Nesta. "But I won't. Are you sure these needles are sterilized properly, Luce? We might get some horrible disease. I don't think it's safe to share blood."

"Chicken," I said.

"Oh, come on you big sissy," said T. J., taking the needle from her. "I'll do it for you."

"No, no," she cried, rolling over on the floor on top of her hands. "You'll stab me or hit an artery or something."

"Trust me. I'm a doctor," said T. J. "Or at least my parents are."

"No," said Nesta, getting up again. "I'll do it myself." Once again, she softly prodded her thumb with the needle. "No. . . . It's not working. No. Sorry. Can't do it."

"Well, we can't carry on if you don't," said Lucy. "It wouldn't be right. Me, T. J., and Izzie would be bonded for life and you'd be on the outside. It might be awful bad luck."

"Yeah, come on, cowardy custard," I said, massaging my thumb. "My blood's drying up."

"I'm sorry, I can't. I just can't." Nesta leaned back

and grabbed the spell book off the bed. "Isn't there some other thing we can do to bond us for life? Something that doesn't involve pain?" She reached for the Pringles. "How about we all take a bite of one of these and pass it on. Bond over a Pringle. Same sort of thing-caring sharing, bonding schmonding."

I had to laugh. Nesta never takes anything like doing spells seriously. "Go on, then. Pass us a Pringle," I said.

Nesta selected one from the tub, then we passed it around, each taking a tiny bite of it.

"Okay, by the power vested in me by this salt and vinegar crisp," I said in my best solemn voice, "I hereby decree that these four girls gathered here tonight shall be friends for ever and ever, bound together by the magical force of the Almighty Pringle."

Lucy and Nesta started laughing. "All hail to the Pringle," said Lucy.

"All hail," T. J. and I echoed.

Then I had an idea. "Okay, then how about this? If we really want to have an experience that will bond us, how about doing something that will look good as well?"

"What do you mean?" asked T. J. "Like dressing up to do spells?"

"No. How about we get our belly buttons pierced?"

There was a stunned silence. I don't think they expected anything like that, but I'd been thinking about having it done for a while. Part of a whole new image. We were going into Year Ten at school a week on Monday and somehow I wanted to leave the old Izzie behind with the old year. I felt like I'd grown out of so many of the things I'd been into, including my clothes-literally with some of them. I seemed to have shot up a few more inches over the last year and some of my jeans were stopping short of my ankles. Très uncool. Anyway, I'd told Mum that I was having a midteen crisis and needed some new clothes. She'd laughed and said there was no such thing as a midteen crisis, as when you're a teen, it's crisis all the way-mainly for her. Poo. I don't think she knows how lucky she is. If she knew what some of the girls at our school get up to behind their parents' backs, she'd have a fit. Relatively, I give her an easy time, although she doesn't think so.

"Hmm," said Nesta finally. "Having a stud put in will probably hurt as well, won't it? But . . . I have always wanted one." She stroked her impossibly flat tummy. "Yeah, a belly button stud would look neat."

"It won't hurt," I said. "Candice Carter had hers done. She was telling me earlier this evening at the party. She said they put stuff on your tummy that kind of freezes it so you don't feel anything."

"Well, I'm in," said Lucy. "I need all the help I can get, to get boys to notice me. A belly button stud would look really cool and might detract from the fact that I have no basoomas."

"Basoomas?" asked T. J. "What are they?"

Lucy pointed at her chest. "Boobs, you idiot. Lal calls them basoomas or jaloobis."

T. J. pulled a face. "He needs help, your brother does."

"Tell me about it," sighed Lucy.

"We could all have a different color stone on our stud," I said. "Have you got any books on astrology, Lucy?"

"Course," she said, getting up and going to her shelf. "That one you gave me last Christmas."

When she handed me the book, I had a quick flick through and found a section on which stones and colors are right for different signs. "Okay, here it is, our birthstones. It says garnet for those born in January, so that's me."

"What color is a garnet?" asked Lucy.

"Sort of deep wine red," I answered.

Lucy nodded approvingly. "That would look good on you with your dark hair."

"Nesta, you're Leo," I continued, "so it says . . . let me see . . . you were born August eighteen, so yours would be a ruby. Wow, that would look fab against your dark skin. Really exotic."

"Nah," said Nesta shaking her head. "I'd look like some belly dancer. No. I want a diamond if I'm going to have anything. Much classier."

"Fine, whatever," I said. "Lucy. Gemini, born May twenty-four. . . . It says emerald for you."

"An emerald might look better on you, Izzie," said Nesta, "to go with your green eyes."

"Yeah. I'd rather have a sapphire," said Lucy.

"You know, blue, to match my eyes."

"Yeah, and blue suits blonds," said Nesta.

"Well, we don't have to stick to this," I said. "It's just if we wanted our birthstones."

"What's mine?" asked T. J.

I flicked through the book to Sagittarius. "Okay, November to December. It says November, topaz, December, turquoise. You were born November twenty-four, so topaz. It'd be great."

"Topaz? That's yellow, isn't it?" asked T. J. "I don't think that's a good color for a belly button stud at all. You know how some of them go a bit ucky-a yellow stone might look like a lump of solid puss or something."

"Er, T. J., g-ross," laughed Nesta. "But I think you're right. I think a turquoise would look better on a brunette like you."

I closed the book, put the back of my hand on my forehead and sighed my best tragic sigh. "I despair. Sometimes I wonder why I bother with you ignoramuses. I just thought we could be the Birthstone Belly Button Gang, that's all."

"You're mad, Izzie," laughed Lucy. "But it would

be nice if we all got different colors."

T. J. was looking dubious. "I don't know. You lot have all got really flat tummies, but mine's rounded. I don't think they look as good if your stomach isn't like a washboard. Besides, won't it cost a fortune? I don't think I'll have enough, with the pocket money I get."

"Good point," said Lucy. "Cost-what do you think?"

"I'll find out," I said. "I doubt it will be that much. I mean, it's not like we're buying real diamonds and gold or anything."

T. J. still looked anxious. "I don't think my mum and dad will like it."

"They don't need to see it," said Nesta. "We're going back to school in just over a week. Soon we'll be in winter clothes. No one will see it."

"So what's the point of having one done?" asked T. J.

"When we're out together, stupid," said Nesta. "When we wear crop tops."

"I guess," said T. J.

"So we all in?" I asked.

The others nodded, T. J. somewhat reluctantly.

"Right then," I said. "Tomorrow morning. I've seen a place in Kentish Town near where the band plays. We'll go there."

Mates, Dates, and Mad Mistakes

Available May 2004
from Simon Pulse

Check Your PULSE Book Club

Sign up for the CHECK YOUR PULSE
free teen e-mail book club!

 ★ FEATURING ★

A new book discussion every month

Monthly book giveaways

Chapter excerpts

Book discussions with the authors

Literary horoscopes

Plus YOUR comments!

To sign up go to www.simonsays.com/simonpulse and
don't forget to CHECK YOUR PULSE!